Seconds of Pleasure

◈

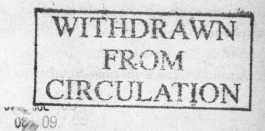

Seconds of Pleasure

Stories

◆

Neil LaBute

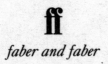

faber and faber

This book is for Elvis Costello

Contents

◈

some do it naturally
some obscenely
everywhere.

—Charles Bukowski

"Who in this world knows anything of
any other heart—or of his own?"

—Ford Madox Ford

Seconds of Pleasure

◆

Perfect

◈

Look, I'm not perfect. That's the important thing here, that you know that, before we begin. I am not perfect. Not even close. In fact, I'm barely average, if anything. I'm just this extremely basic guy who goes pretty much unnoticed most of the time. I say "most" of the time because of course there are moments in a day when I stand out; of course there are, everybody has those. But usually, I mean, for the most part, I'm nothing special. I just go along, doing my thing, no problem.

I'm valuable at work, dependable and pleasant, and a man who is generally seen as "going places." Not that

I'm a slave to the office, mind you; I'm not one of those. No. I'm there on time—"on the dot," as my father used to say—often stay a little into the evening but try to take a good hour or so out for lunch. Walk around the park or through the mall over on Beacon when the weather turns. If you don't do that, get out and stretch the legs, I mean, you're just asking for trouble. Begging for it. And in those places—the park, the mall, any of the nearby restaurants—I move happily and anonymously about. Oh sure, I see the occasional coworker, but a wave of the hand and a "hey there" usually do the trick. Sometimes there's a few minutes of shoptalk or gossip, but I try to keep that noon hour reserved mostly for ol' number one. I think it's added years to my life. I really do. I don't often socialize with my office mates, either, not anymore. I used to, when I first started out there, but that whole after-hours scene has really cooled down for me. See, I'm married. Yep, got myself hitched about two years ago now and it's great, it really is, but marriage takes up a lot of time and energy if you do it right. That's what they tell me, anyway. A solid marriage is a real commitment. And I plunged in feetfirst, believe you me. I really did. Once I met her, "woman of my dreams" and all that, well, it just didn't make sense to do anything but go for it.

See, I was quite the bachelor in my day. Oh yeah. Not that I had a series of amorous exploits or anything like that, some big Casanova deal going, but I had my fair share of adventures. A lady or two picked up in a local club, some moments from my student life that might be better off relived. Or forgotten. A couple hearts broken, no doubt, trampled and left in the ditch along the road-side of love. You know the one I'm talking about—that little ravine there that collects corsages and condoms and discarded socks. Yes, a few of my exes landed squarely in that wretched place. One even ended her life, I'm sorry to say. Committed suicide, and in a rather unpleasant way, too. Stepped in front of a bus, an oncoming bus, and was hit straight on, meaning that she just had time to turn fully toward the driver, probably got her hands in the air—that classic pose, you know the one, like Cary Grant in that movie at Mount Rushmore, like that—before it hit her and dragged her halfway down the next city block. It was a woman driver in the bus, a female driver. Not that that had anything to do with it, the accident; I just felt I should point it out. Get the facts straight. No, it was her fault completely, from all reports. My ex-girlfriend's. Several onlookers saw the whole thing, witnessed it, and each story was remarkably consistent. She had stood there—Patsy was her name, she was called "Patsy"—and waited patiently for the uptown express, watched several other buses pass, in fact, before moving quickly and purposefully out in front of the No. 6. No doubt about it, Patsy had killed herself and that was that. Not that it had anything to do with me, God no. I mean, not really. Yes, we had fought earlier that week—an attempt at reconciliation had ended in a brutal shouting match in the International House of Pancakes—and several phone calls between us had been equally painful, but I feel in no way responsible for what happened to her. It was simply her time. Or she had simply made time, I guess, is more like it. I suppose when you kill yourself, it has more to do with setting up an appointment with Destiny than Destiny showing up unannounced. No, Patsy had thoughtfully called ahead and Destiny had penciled her in. The fact that she had chosen the uptown 6—the bus that she would ride to my apartment, the one that runs near the river rather than out past the station and then back over—simply added a layer of irony to the proceedings. A fairly healthy layer, actually. Or, as my dad whispered in my ear at the viewing, "This is why I take cabs."

But that's the past, right? And the past is called that for a reason. Because it is behind us, which is good enough for me. No, I try to live in the present. Live in it, work in it, be in it. I-am-present. And presently, what's bothering me is this. It's, well, how can I put this? Delicately, I suppose. That's the only way to do it, I will put it delicately. It's that thing, that skin thing on my wife's body, that is what's bothering me. Haunting me, really. That growth. Now, it's a fine time to bring this up, some physical complaint about my partner, I know that, but I swear I never saw it when we first met, back when we were going out. I'm sure that I didn't. I had no idea that it even existed then, back in our courting days. Not that I didn't see the woman naked; of course I did, on many occasions. But it was often dark, at night, in the heat of passionate embrace. Plus, I wasn't giving the woman an examination, for God's sake—the once-over, as my parents' generation might affectionately call it—so I don't feel that I can be held responsible for missing it in the beginning. Hell, it may not have even been there, now that I think about it. It might've sprouted recently like some new-forming island, erupting from the deep to settle and flourish on her shoulder there. Well, not technically her shoulder, but that fleshy stretch that runs from said shoulder to the side of her neck. Right there. I mean, come to think of it, the number of times I saw her in sleeveless shirts and swimsuits, her wedding dress even, it seems unfathomable that I could've missed this outcropping, this mound of darkened cells that brings me such distress.

Pitiful, you say? Insipid and facile, not to mention shallow? I agree. I completely agree with you that it isn't rational or loving or even very grown-up, but that doesn't alter the fact that it bugs the shit out of me. Almost pathologically so. That wart cluster on my wife's flesh is slowly, methodically killing me. It really is.

I first noticed it last summer, right around the Fourth, I guess, as we were getting ready for a little holiday blowout that my company throws every year up at the lake. You know, that lake just outside the city limits that still has a few trees surrounding it. Not really the country, but as close as we come to it around here. Anyway, we were getting ourselves together for that and I was coming out of my closet—I remember this quite distinctly—and I spotted the offending flap from across the room. I mean, spotted it like a drifting sailor notices land appearing on the vast horizon.

"Hey, what's that?"

"What?" she says, twirling around like a spider has just dropped onto her forearm from above.

"That. Right there."

"Stop it, what?"

"Honey, *that*. Right there on your . . ."

"*Where?*" She jerks about again, backing toward me and swinging her head over to get a look. Straining.

"It's right there . . ."

To be fair, the little clump rests just out of her eye-shot. It would take a courageous twist to the right, then a glance back into a mirror to get a look at where I'm pointing. Which she does.

"Oh, that."

"Yeah, that. There. What is it?"

"I've always had that."

"No, you haven't."

"Yes, I have. Of course I have. Since I was a kid."

"Come on, seriously."

"I think I know my own body."

"Sure, of course, but . . . that has not always been . . ."

"It has! Stop it now, we have to get ready."

And with that she pulls on this flimsy tank top—some kind of silky Anne Klein thing that is no doubt expensive

and made by unfortunate people in another country somewhere and an essential wardrobe item for today's woman—
but it's got no arms on it. Or "sleeves"—whatever you call
them. None. I'm fighting my bare feet into a pair of driving moccasins when I realize this and casually try to steer
the conversation back to the subject at hand.

"Did you get your hair styled or something?"

"No, why?"

"No reason. It just seems . . ."

"What?"

"I dunno. It's lying on your shoulders differently,
maybe that's it."

"That's what? What're you going on about?"

"I'm just asking."

She stops suddenly, really studying me for the first
time all morning. "Is that what you're wearing?"

"Yeah, why?"

"Umm, no reason. No, it's fine."

"I like this shirt."

"Well, that's good."

"Fine, I'll change." I can see where this thing is going
and there is absolutely no chance of winning, none, and
so it's back to the walk-in I go. I call out from deep in the

"short sleeve" section, just down from "sweatshirts" and "sportswear." "What about a light yellow stripe?"

"That's OK, if it's the canary one. Or just white, and then throw a sweater over your shoulders."

I obey and pull down a newer Ralph Lauren when an idea hits me. Straight on, like a piano dropping from the sky in one of those old silent movies—I shall teach by example. Yes indeed. I shuffle over to the "long sleeves" area and grab a Nautica off the rack. Button it down in record time and toss a cranberry pullover on for good measure. I'm set. I walk back out into our bedroom to face my wife as she's finishing her eye makeup. Applying a bit of mascara. And, of course, she's still in the tank top. I'm about to speak but she beats me to it, one eye fluttering as she brushes that little ebony wand across it.

"Aren't you gonna be hot?"

"No, it's by the water."

"Yeah, but it's a lake. An inland lake."

"Right, but . . ."

"It's not like we're going to the *ocean* or something."

"I know that . . ."

"Whatever. Do what you want."

I look at her shoulder again, that god-awful blemish standing at attention and practically winking at me. The strap of her top keeps catching the edge of it, sometimes even snagging it and getting itself hooked there on the craggy tip. OK, no barbecue for me, I guess. I'm about to throw up.

"Aren't you going to grab a cardigan or anything? A little jacket?"

"No, I'm fine."

"You sure? There's gonna be fireworks. We'll be out late . . ."

"I said no, now come on, let's go. We still need to put the deviled eggs in the car, plus the lawn chairs."

"Right, right. OK. I just thought that . . ."

And that's when she catches me. Staring at it. Damn it.

"It bothers you, doesn't it?"

"What?"

"Oh, please!"

"I don't know what you're talking about."

I do a complete reversal here, right on the spot, acting as if I don't know what she's talking about. It's an old tactic—medieval, I think—that is so obvious and silly that most women fall for it, or simply let it go in utter exasperation. At the moment, I use it as my only viable option.

"Yes, you do, of course you do! You know EXACTLY what I'm talking about! Why you haven't said anything about it before *now* I don't get, but whatever . . ."

"Honey, *what?* Why're you acting all . . . ?"

"Just don't. Don't do that."

"I'm not . . ."

"It bugs you so much, fine, I'll wear a . . . it's just a *mole,* for God's sake!"

Now how do I play this? Do I acknowledge what we're talking about, or continue playing dumb because that's more believable—guys are usually at their finest when playing dumb. Trust me on that tiny bit of information.

"It doesn't bother me, not at all. I just asked what it was."

"Please, it totally bothers you."

"Uh-uh. Nope. Come on, let's go." I even make a little move toward the door to prove how open I am to her bringing her "little friend" to the party with us, but she's not buying it. "I'll go get the chairs out of the garage."

"Well, just get one because I'm not going."

"Honey, please, come on . . ."

"I'm not," and with that the tank is pulled over her head and off. She smirks as she throws it onto the bed, turning to me in her faded pink brassiere.

"Sweetie, I wasn't . . ."

"Satisfied now?"

I stare long and hard at her chest for a moment—not her best feature—trying to gather my thoughts. I lose myself in her cleavage, mostly because it allows me to avoid her eyes while absently noticing that both breasts have dropped another quarter inch or so since the last time I studied them—the right one perhaps slightly more than the other. I also spot that dusky birthmark just outside the ring of her left nipple (which I always thought looked like the state of Ohio but never said a word about it to her). A flash suddenly goes through my head of freshman English back at Pepperdine, where some teaching assistant forced us to read that Nathaniel Hawthorne guy. A short story of his that had to do with some flaw in an otherwise lovely woman, but I can't remember any of the specifics about it for the life of me. Not with her glaring at me, anyway. The missus.

"If that's what you want, then fine."

"It's what you want!"

"No, it isn't." I see the broken bottle of an argument at our feet and try to step gingerly around it. "It was just a question."

"Don't lie."

"I'm not lying!" And I don't feel as if I am, not really. Not at this specific moment, at least. "Honestly, I'm not."

"Just go without me, I'm tired now."

"Well, OK, if you want me to . . ."

"See, I knew you didn't want me to come!"

"Jesus, please, I don't wanna do this right now! I asked you one thing, *one,* and you get all nuts on me here . . ."

"Go, then, I don't care! Just GO!!" And with that she swings around and marches off to the bathroom, slamming the door behind her. Slams it so hard that an actual cracking sound is made when the latch catches on the jam. With her gone for a moment, I can freely roll my eyes and check my hair before walking over to make the obvious and required plea for her to forgive me and join me at the event. I do it, that little dance near the wall—calling out her name a few times and then promising her the world. Thankfully, she's pretty angry with me and stays put. Mission accomplished.

The drive out to the park at the north end of the lake affords me some time to run through these events and

review my behavior. Was I out of line? Could I have be-
haved differently? Well, of course I could've, but what's
done is done. The whole episode is already receding into
the past for me and you know how I feel about that. The
past. Before I can get too lost in "who's to blame?" or
"should I call and circle back?" I see the hand-painted
signs and balloons that mark the route to a makeshift
parking area. Twenty minutes later I'm on the front lines
of our annual volleyball game and I don't give that earlier ordeal another thought.

   It's been several years now since the events I've just
described and I'm happy to say that my wife and I are
still together. She is essentially a good woman, and despite a rough patch or two, our married life has been
pretty much OK. "Clear sailing," as my uncle used to
say (a man who never sailed a day in his life). Never
again have I mentioned the offending mark on my wife's
body, to her or to anyone else. I also refrain from sug-
gesting more appropriate clothing choices, conceal-
ing makeup, or cosmetic surgery. On occasion, I even
run my fingers across it, very casually, to let her know
that I do not fear the thing or worry about it in the
slightest.

But sometimes, some days when I'm walking through the mall or out near one of my other personal spots at lunch, I have a vision. I do. A rather elaborate dream where I find myself holding her down, pinning my own wife down on the wooden floor of our bedroom at, say, midnight, catching her groggy and off guard as I plunge a potato peeler or something else suitably sharp into the offending mound and tear it from her body. It's only a fantasy, of course, but it has the color and fury of vivid reality in my head. Her, fighting and clawing me as I push her face into the parquet, a handful of nightgown in my fist as I work that kitchen tool deep into her shoulder. Burrowing in. Finally, yes, finally freeing her and myself of that thing. That imagined creature that has come so deliberately between us.

I would never do this, of course, and it's important for you to understand that. I could never act on such an impulse, heavens no, but these are my thoughts and they can't always be controlled because I am not perfect, as mentioned before. I am just not perfect. All I know is that occasionally now, more than once in a while, I'm over-taken by an image or flash from the above scenario and I'll completely lose track of time—find myself down by the old band shell or God knows where, nearly two in the afternoon. Drifting. Just drifting.

Am I concerned about this behavior? Frightened, even? Yes, I am, yes. Obviously so. But in my defense I must say this: When I do have one of those "moments," I mean an all-out episode like I've been having of late, I always return to my work with the snap and vigor of a man reborn.

Maraschino

◈

It was good to see him again. Really, it was. He hadn't actually changed a lot; I mean, not that much. A little, I guess, but I spotted him immediately. Almost, anyway. Just a couple minutes after he walked in. He did have some sort of exotic-type drink in his hands, a "Typhoon Betty" or something, so I suppose he must've been inside long enough to buy that, but I caught his eye a second later. He was nibbling on the cherry—I forget the name of those, what is it?—you know, the one from his glass, when we looked at each other. Anyway, we had one of those, like, "things" across the room. We did, honestly.

The kind from a TV movie or something. He saw me. I'd already seen him, as I said. And we just stared at each other, must've been around four minutes at least. Music blaring. People up and moving around the place—you know what the lounge in a Holiday Inn can be like on a Wednesday—but we didn't feel any of it. I didn't, anyhow. It was suddenly just him and me. I was only in town for a day and a half, flying to Sacramento on Friday morning, early, so you know, not exactly expecting a blast from the past. And yet there he was. Cherry stem in his mouth and staring straight at me. It was obvious he didn't recognize me outright, but I must've struck a chord or something, the angle of his body as he stood there, head cocked a little to one side, and that half smile. But I guess he couldn't place me. Which is OK, it'd been a while, and I'm sure I looked different in a business suit. See, I work for a big pharmacy chain, in marketing, so I need to have "the look." You know, keep the corporate thing going . . . so that was probably part of it.

As he talks to me, I realize pretty quick that this isn't his first drink, not even his third, so no wonder he doesn't remember me. The face or any of it. But he's smiling throughout. Not a cheap, kind of irritating smile, but the real kind. A "smile" smile. Chatting me up about who I work for, when I graduated, brand of bra. You know, the usual. Not slurring the words yet, but a stumble or two. When he whispers my cup size back to me I'm suddenly a 63C . . . now, maybe he's dyslexic, but I don't think so. A simple mistake, I figure; it's the drink talking. I understand this, so I just grin, grin back at him and answer dutifully on everything he asks. Wondering if something I say will set off a bell in his head, maybe a whistle. Just a flicker even, somewhere in those tired, distant eyes of his.

Sitting there on the bed of his junior suite, twenty minutes later, I'm still half hoping he'll remember me. It'd make this a whole bunch easier. Well, not easier, I suppose, but more like a reunion than some other kind of thing. Doesn't really matter, I guess, but it'd certainly be interesting. As close as he comes is that I remind him of someone. He says this, more to himself than anything, as he's pulling off his socks. You know, the thin, stretchy kind. He tugs at one reinforced toe as he stares at my belly button, eyes traveling down as he mumbles a name. I ask who she is, the name, say that I won't be offended. But he turns back to his heel and says that it's nothing. No one. Some lady from when he was younger, an ex-wife when I press him. I promise myself right then that if he spots me, figures it out somehow, a gesture or the way I raise my eyebrows, even, anything, then I'll let him go. But he doesn't. So I don't.

It's funny, lying there, letting him fuck me like that. Well, maybe not funny, exactly, but different. He looks down from time to time, studying my mouth, but mostly he just grunts and sighs and pushes on. At one point, he asks me to turn over, to try it that way, but I resist and tell him I like looking at him, so eventually he closes his eyes and gets on with it. Near the end, his body tensing, I wonder if he used to fuck her like this, my mother. I saw them once, doing it, I mean, but I was really too young to recall much. And did he fuck that first woman he left us for this way? Or the second wife? Who knows? Not me, I was only six. I'm still wondering this as I pull my blazer back on, run a hand through my hair, and kiss his cheek. We lock eyes again, I give him a last chance, but nothing; he's too busy with those socks of his. Oh, he does check the corridor for me, though. That was nice. Opens the door a few inches, a towel around his heavy waist, and then out I go.

I turn only once, when I reach the safety of the ice machine, but a nod is all we muster. No need for a hallway promise, an exchange of business cards, some half-forgotten e-mail address. No. Just a smile and that's enough. It's kind of far away, but I'd swear he opens his mouth again to speak. He stops, though, stops himself, probably catching another woman's name on his tongue. My mom's? Someone else's? Doesn't matter. Anyway, it was good to see him again. Really, it was.

Time-Share

◆

He stands there, dripping, with his head tipped down a bit. Just a bit, but hoping that this slight tilting forward of his eyes will prove that he is sorry. Very sorry. Repentant.

"Say that again," she says, after studying him. Watching.

"What, about before?"

"Yes, that. Please."

"Well, see, we, ummm . . ." He creeps forward cautiously with this next thought. True, she seems less hysterical now, ready to listen, but who knows? ". . . the two of us had actually met before."

"Before?"

"I mean, before *we* met." He thinks about this for a moment, about the genesis of the thing. "From before we, that is you and I, knew one another."

"Really?"

"Yeah. We went to the same college and . . ."

"Oh. So . . . you were in school together?"

"No, no, not *together*. It was in Kansas, but not overlapping or anything. No, we actually ran into each other in the city one time, during this coed softball game of alumni in Central Park."

"Quaint."

"Which is kind of funny . . ."

"Why? Why is that funny?"

"Well, it's, you know . . . Manhattan."

"Uh-huh."

"And that's where we went to school, too. Manhattan, I mean. In Kansas. Because Kansas State is in . . ."

"Yeah, Manhattan. I get it," she says, without changing expressions. "It's just not that funny."

"Right," he acknowledges, then moves ahead.

"Anyway, that's where we were, over by the softball fields, and, see, we got talking about stuff, had a couple drinks, you know, and we just hung out a few times or whatever."

"I think they still call it 'dating,' even in New York."

"No it wasn't like a '*thing*'! We didn't date or anything, we just . . ."

"Slept together."

". . . something like that." He falters a bit but plows on, spitting out the truth. Well, part of it, anyway. "Yeah, this one time we did, yes. Do that, I mean. Not *sleeping* together, though, just some sex stuff. Sort of. But it was nothing . . ."

"So that makes it all right, then . . . what I saw."

"No, not all right, I'm not saying that, I just mean . . ." He considers where to go next, what minefields to avoid and which to blunder off into. ". . . hell, I dunno, just that there's some background there. A shared background between us."

"Right. I see." She responds quickly, in small, staccato bursts of language, rather than really thinking through her next sentence. "I get it. I do. I do get it."

"So, it's not like, I mean . . . a 'fling' or anything."

"It isn't?!"

"Well, OK, yes, a fling, but . . . a fling with qualifi-
ers. With *history*." He throws the last part in just for effect, the history bit, but hoping that it sticks somehow.

"You didn't tell me, though. About this 'history' of
yours, I mean. All this time and you didn't say anything."

"No, I didn't do that."

"Why?"

"I thought that I wouldn't, you know . . ."

"Uh-uh, no, I don't know. What?" Then she realizes.
"Get caught?"

"No." He stutters twice before saying, "B-b-be
understood."

"Well, you're right, you wouldn't b-b-be," she says,
obviously mocking him.

"See?"

"But that shouldn't stop you from telling me!" She
says this louder than she means to, but it's out now. Hangs
there in the air for a moment, her dark cloud of disbelief, then drifts off.

"What was I gonna say?"

"I don't know, it's not really my moral dilemma,
is it?"

"It's not a . . ." He thinks carefully now, a misstep
here could be fatal. There's definitely some sort of

morality involved in having sex with your neighbors, he muses. ". . . OK, yeah, it is, like, a *moral* thing, but I think we can still . . ."

"Still what? What?!" She stops for a moment, stops loading clothes into her flowered Laura Ashley day bag and turns to him. Faces him directly. "I'd love to hear how that sentence ends. Tell me."

". . . work something out? Or . . ." He tries to hold her gaze but can't. If he wasn't wearing his Tommy Hilfiger swim trunks he might have a fighting chance, but standing there in this moist orange suit it's just not possible. He looks away and out a window, catching a hint of the gray Cape Cod next door. Their place. The neighbors'.

"You think we should work it out, do you? Is that what you think?"

"I think we could try."

"Try what, talking? Just, like, *talking*, you and me?"

"We could, yes. That would be . . ."

"What about therapy?" she challenges back. "Or how about just sharing, the two of us and the two of them? The four of us could swing on various nights, try new positions. How's that sound?" She studies him a moment, but he can't meet her eyes. "Probably great, doesn't it? I mean, if you're not too possessive, that is. And then once we've paired up the kids we'll all be just one big, happy family!"

"If we can't talk about this like adults, then we might as well . . ."

"Adults? Oh, you wanna talk like *ad*-ults, is that what you'd like?"

"It's why I came back over here, yes."

"No, you came back over because this is your house, OK, this is your *home*. Where you live!" She throws a handful of perfumes in on top of her blouses, the bottles clinking dully together in the sea of fabric. The sound itself is not very impressive, not as resounding as she'd hoped for, but she'd needed to pack them anyway. "What'd you think, you could just live in the pool house there, set up a little place for yourselves or something?"

"No. Of course not."

"Then what?"

"Look, I don't know what you think you saw . . ."

"Oh, please, come on . . ."

"No, seriously, what? We weren't . . ."

"Your trunks were down, all right?"

"They weren't . . ." He doesn't finish this because she moves toward him now. Quickly across the room to challenge what he'll say next. "OK, whatever. You know what you know."

"No, not whatever. I saw you, very clearly, your Tommy suit around your knees and your big white ass pointed right at me. Your back was toward the door and your thing was . . . do you really wanna hear more?"

". . . no."

"I saw it out. I did."

"Not *out,* no, it was just caught in my . . ." He tries to mime an explanation but a wagging finger from her stops him cold.

"When you turned, surprised by the door and turning quickly, I know I saw your . . . thing . . . out of your suit. It got tangled in your mesh, there in the white mesh when you tried to hide it away. I know what I'm saying . . ."

"But . . . we knew each other in New York . . ."

"What does that mean?! You keep saying that but it doesn't seem to mean anything. *Lots* of people know each other in the city, but that doesn't mean they're all doing it. Does it?"

"No, but, see . . . we went to the same college and we got talking one time, we had a lot to drink and we just . . . it wasn't like this big thing."

"But you didn't tell me."

"No."

"They've been moved in there, next door, in their time-share for three weeks. A month maybe. Since Memorial Day . . ."

"I was going to say something . . ."

"But you decided to keep it all to yourself, huh?"

"No! God, you're so . . . we were both nervous about it. I mean, embarrassed."

"Obviously . . ."

"We were! When they introduced themselves that first day, out there on the deck, I could hardly look up . . ."

"Or just now . . ."

"That's what I'm saying . . ."

". . . of course, you were a little busy."

"Stop! Jesus, let me at least tell my side of it."

"Please . . . go ahead."

"So, you know . . . if you don't take that moment, I mean, that first moment there and tell the truth, then you're stuck. You are."

"Like your thing in the mesh . . ."

"A little, yes . . ." He wants to smile, since that was pretty funny, especially for her, but he can't risk it. Not right now. It might not have been a joke. Instead, he offers, "Kind of like that. Uh-huh."

"And since you didn't tell me out on the porch that day, you just figured this tiny detail was no big thing. I mean, not a real problem for us . . . is that kind of what you're saying?"

"Sort of . . ."

"Huh."

"What's that mean?"

"Just 'huh,' no other real meaning to it . . ." Her head cocks a touch now, slightly to one side as she studies him. Glancing at his eyes but then down, to settle at crotch level. Holding this look for quite some time. He shifts from one bare foot to the other.

"What're you doing?"

"Nothing."

"No, seriously, what?"

"Just imagining . . ."

"Imagining?" He waits for her next volley, stepping off the wet spot he's created and involuntarily moving away from her. She takes her time.

"Imagining what it'd be like for your son to walk into that shed. Looking for, oh, I dunno, some diving sticks or an *inner tube* or who knows what, and see that. What I saw . . ."

"What? We knew each other in Manhattan . . ."

"Stop saying *that!*" She glares at him, obviously con-juring up a picture. "How would it be for him to see your . . . cock—there, do you like that better? You're always wanting me to talk dirty, does that sound better?—to see his daddy's *cock* out and . . ."

"We were just talking . . ."

"Please don't do that! Don't assume I've been near-sighted all these years on top of being an idiot . . ."

". . . it was this boys versus girls softball game we were in, that's where we first . . ."

"Would you like it, if he saw that?"

"No."

"You wouldn't?"

"Of course not . . ."

"Well, that's something . . ."

"But I wouldn't . . . and I'm not trying to start anything here . . . no offense, but I wouldn't want him to see it in anyone's mouth. I mean, including yours." He almost gri-maces after that one, not sure he didn't just step into some abyss.

"Then perhaps you should stop sticking it *in* people's mouths . . . shouldn't you?"

". . . yeah. I mean, yes, you're right." That's the least he can say. She does have a point there, albeit a fairly simple mathematical one.

"So, it was *in*, then?" She waits.

". . . what?"

"You had your thing out and in . . ."

"Yes." Better to cut his losses now, mercy of the court and all that. "I did, yes, for just, like, a second. A moment is all. Honestly."

"Oh."

"Yeah . . ."

"Because I couldn't really see . . . my eyes hadn't adjusted. I was pretty sure that's what was happening there, with the two of you, but I wasn't completely. Certain, I mean. Because of the dark. But, hey, now I know . . ." She smiles weakly, finally matching one of his more pathetic grins at the same instant. "I only went in there looking for their tiki torches. They told me we could use them for the barbecue on Saturday. That's why I . . . anyway . . ."

"Listen, we were just . . ."

"Right."

"You know?"

"Yeah, college, I know . . ."

"Exactly."

"The big game and all."

"Yep . . ." He fixates on a framed picture for a moment, drifting. A Hopper print of someone sitting in a room somewhere. Alone. Lucky bastard, he thinks to himself.

"I see."

". . . I mean, you're in the city, right? And you run into a bunch of folks from home, you know, men and women out there on the grass having fun, and you just sort of get caught up in the thing . . . few beers . . . I can't really explain it better than that . . ." He tries to, though, for a minute at least, his mouth searching for a more perfect phrase. It doesn't come.

"OK."

"Does that make any sense?"

"No, none." She shrugs, unwilling to say more.

"Oh . . ."

"But I understand. I understand that it makes sense to you . . . somehow."

"It does. I know it sounds wobbly, but . . ."

"And since it does, make sense, I mean, you'll need to explain it to them . . ."

"Who?"

"The children."

". . . what do you mean?"

"You're going to need to sit them down—they're back from swimming in forty minutes—and you'll need to walk them through this as best you can."

"No, I can't . . . what?"

"My leaving, I mean. You'll need to come up with something for that. Tell them the rest if you want to, but you have to explain where I've gone."

"But where are you . . . ?"

"To the city, I suppose. For the night, anyway. I need to call my sister, and the lawyers, no doubt." She seems to tower over him at this moment, although she is only five feet three and not wearing heels, not even the espadrilles he'd bought her at that Wal-Mart on the way in. "I need to handle a few things."

"I can't tell them that! I mean, they're only . . ."

"What, children?"

"Yes."

"Children bounce back. They do, that's their lot in life."

"Wait . . ."

"You explain things and on Saturday we'll get them on a train, back into town, and they'll be out of your hair."

She smiles some inner smile at this. "Then you can go back over the fence . . ."

"But I don't want to."

"Then don't."

"I want to . . . I mean, I'd like to, I'd really like to see if we could . . ."

"What?" She waits for him to finish but he only repeats the previous phrases over and over. Trying to jumpstart a solution but never getting past the opening. Finally, she picks up her bag, tests the weight of it, then moves toward the door. He doesn't stop her.

"Do you want me to carry that down or . . . ?"

"No, no, it's fine. You've done enough, believe me . . ."

"I love you guys. I do." He didn't want to have to pull that one out, not at this late date but he goes for it. Pitches the love thing out there like a final horseshoe.

"Well, that's something you can hang on to, isn't it? You can tell the kids that, if it helps . . . tell them I love them, too."

"We were just talking . . . we spent time on the same *campus,* for Chrissakes!"

"Yeah, I caught that part . . ."

"We did . . ."

"I know."

"And we had some . . ."

"When did you become so pathetic?" This isn't meant to be rhetorical.

". . . I'm not sure."

"Huh." She stands at the door now, flicking the light switch off more from habit than anything. He pulls his arms in and around his exposed upper body now, stands in the semidark staring at his departing wife. She starts down a step then turns back, rotates even, and comes into the room again. "Tell me one thing . . ."

"Yes?"

"Just one."

"OK."

"What position did he play?"

"Huh?"

"Our *neighbor* . . . the guy who was sucking your dick." This is new for her, this strong language thing, and she seems to be enjoying it. "When you met him, what position was he playing?"

"Oh . . . catcher. He was their catcher."

". . . I see." A pause, then a slight smile from her in the gloom.

"You do?"

"I get it now . . ."

"Get what?"

"The significance of it all."

"What do you mean?"

"Come on, he's the *catcher* . . . you don't know anyone, you're lonely, it's New York, this guy's kneeling at your feet, you've got your nice, firm bat there . . . I get it. It's *symbolic* . . ."

"No, come on . . ." He hesitates now, unsure about her. Is she being ironic? "We were just . . ."

"What? You *what*?"

"It . . . it was an experiment, that's all. Just . . . guy stuff. Kind of, like, you know . . ."

"No, you're right. It happens. It does. In 'Manhattan,' anyway . . ."

"We were only . . . see, I met him before we, I mean, you and me . . ."

". . . I hope you're very happy." Before he can say anything else she is gone, the door clicking shut downstairs a moment later. Normally, he would follow her, do the dramatic run down the block to the train station, but he's got the swimsuit on and it would just look ridiculous now. He's sure of that. No, better to talk tomorrow, let things cool down a bit. Take care of the kids, maybe get a bucket of Kentucky Fried Chicken and watch a movie. Face the rest of it in the morning. Yes. That's it.

"It's OK, it is, it's OK, this is gonna be . . . it's all right. Things'll be fine. It's . . . OK, this is all O-K . . ." He says this aloud but more to himself than anything, a kind of masculine mantra as he strips off his damp trunks. He shivers slightly, then begins to wander around the room naked, hunting down a pair of discarded Levi's in the oncoming twilight.

Boo-Boo

◆

They remind him of those girls from that John Updike story, the one about the guy in the supermarket. It's really great, although the title of it doesn't come easily to mind. It has the same name as one of those East Coast stores, probably because he's from up around there. Updike. True, this is a bookstore he's in and there are only two of them—girls, that is—and Updike's little tale had three, but they are the same kind of breed. Cut from the same cloth, as it were. After all, girls will be girls will be girls.

They are both wearing their start-of-summer gear, featuring a T-shirt, shorts, and sneakers. Soon, as the days drag on and the heat starts to get at them, they'll trade this in for tank tops or swimsuits, probably the same shorts—they both wear the cute, girlie kind that's too short and tight for their own good—and flip-flops. But for now, right now, they are content with this. This "look." Besides, neither one seems brave enough to attempt a solo run, a dash for the summit. No. Each outfit appears to have been carefully selected by a committee of two through a series of elaborate phone calls or e-mails that allows for no mishap. In other words, they know exactly what they're doing.

That's what he's thinking, anyway, standing there just off to the side and pretending to read *Art in America* as he studies the tall one's legs. Well, perhaps "study" is too strong a word for what he's doing. That would seem to imply an intense, open sort of examination of his subject, all in the name of science or some other significant goal. No, staring might be more like it. The covert kind of staring, to be precise, of the type practiced by middle-aged men who have no real business or purpose for being in a Barnes & Noble on a Thursday afternoon. That's what he's doing. Staring.

It's not her legs, per se, that interest him, although they are fine and long and brown. Like the gangly appendages of a newborn colt or that one black runner who won a gold medal or two a few years back. He can't recall her name right now, but this gal's lower half is a bit like hers. Or, better yet, like that young woman who lives catty-corner to his house, the one whose parents recently divorced and her mother moved across town so he sees her less frequently now. The daughter, that is. This girl's legs are just like hers. Full of life and youth and promise.

Except for the cut, of course. That's what makes them different. Helps them stand out. It's not a fresh wound, no, but more like a week old or so. He's no authority, obviously, but if he had to venture a guess, say, found himself on a game show with a new Volvo on the line, then he'd probably say a week. What leads him to this, this guess, is the color of the scabbing and the general state of the mark. See, she's already been scratching at the thing, picking at it while she's been on the phone or watching the Disney Channel.

Even now her hand keeps creeping down and flicking at the thin red gash, pulling off bits of skin and blood and rolling them slowly between her thumb and middle finger. And it's white beneath. That's his clue, you see. The flesh is pure and white in the area where she works, leading him to conclude that the abrasion is nearly healed. She is almost whole again. Only the scratching at it betrays her, which is what initially caught his attention. When it did, he quickly replaced the *Maxim* back into its space and drifted over toward the girls. The *Art in America* was simply picked up on the fly. As cover.

He checks himself quickly in the window across the way, moving a bit to one side to get a better look. Out from behind the backward "Noble" painted on the glass. He smiles at his own outline, flashing a mouthful of store-bought teeth. Well, he didn't actually buy the teeth themselves but has purchased the braces that cover them. The clear kind, those little strips of plastic that are only noticeable when you get close enough. From a distance you can barely tell. Barely. He checks one last time—in the hazy reflection, it simply looks as if he forgot to brush this morning—and then moves back to lean on the magazine shelf.

No cheap wire racks in a place like this, either. No. These magazines are all kept on lovely wooden shelves. Except for the "gentlemen's issues," of course, which are held behind the counter and wrapped in heavy plastic.

Which is fine by him, since that's where they belong. And anyhow, if he were to feel the need to make a purchase like that—only a *Playboy* or something equally harmless, never the hard stuff—then he would motor on down to 7-Eleven like any grown man would do and pick up some aspirin or a snack cake or hot sandwich beforehand like it's meant to be done. The magazine in question would simply be an afterthought. Just for fun.

These girls, however, are more than that. Fun. No, this is serious business and he treats it as such. Hunter and prey have a healthy respect for one another, at least in his mind. From where he's standing, these two young ladies are the be-all and end-all of his happy little Thursday. A day out of the office and what a nice surprise this is turning out to be. A smile begins to creep over his face but he quietly tucks it back inside his mouth. He doesn't want a thing like that to give him away—too many house-wives and protective mothers wandering the place to let that happen. He chomps down hard on the fleshy part of his tongue, really digging in with his teeth, and the grin begins to fade. Suddenly, he's back in business.

A drop of blood has gathered on her calf now, at the top of the wound. Nothing very alarming, mind you, simply a spot of red that has gone unchecked for the last few minutes. In fact, you'd really have to be looking to even notice it. But then that's what he's doing, of course. Gawking. He's moved beyond staring, you see, shifted into third, and shot right past staring on the straightaway. He is openly gawking now, and it's anybody's guess how long he can keep it up. He does realize this, of course; he's been doing this long enough to know when he's merely staring and when it becomes more than that. When it makes its way over into the realm of something really special. And this young lady, with her delicious limbs curled up beneath her brushed metal chair, is about as special as any person could ever hope to be. So, so special.

An argument erupts at the checkout stand and the man snaps his head around, sensing that his time is almost up. The raised voices up front belong to his wife—well, one of them, anyway. Sometimes it sounds like she has two voices, actually, the noise that emits from her. It would be hard for anyone, at least the casual passer-by, to believe that so much volume could come from a single person, but he knows better. Oh yes. It's her, all right. He can just make out the finer points of the discussion, something about her Reader's Advantage card being expired and "Would you care to extend your buying power at this time?" or something like that. All he knows is that she, his wife, keeps saying no very loudly and heads are starting to turn. Not the girls, thankfully, as they keep sucking on the straws of their very grown-up iced coffees—to be fair, they're covered in whipped cream and chocolate jimmies—and pointing at photos in an issue of *YM*.

The girl in question takes another dig at her leg and he realizes, very lucidly, that it is pretty much now or never. A flash goes off in his head, a snapshot of a film that he saw years ago, in college maybe, of a man obsessed with a young woman's leg. Her knee or something. One of those French or Italian kinds, where not much happens and the words are carefully printed all along the bottom of the screen. It was one of those. He can't recall much else about it, except that this perfectly respectable guy is dying to touch some blond girl's leg. Various other hijinks ensue along the way, no doubt, but that's the plot in a nutshell—an older fellow touching the leg of this youngster. And it happens, he touches it, so at least it had a happy ending. He doesn't know all that much about foreign films, but the ones that he's seen often seem to end badly. Maybe that's why he remembers this one; the conclusion is a happy affair.

The coins spill from his hand in a casual enough manner. They hit the faux marble and scatter in a predictable pattern, shooting off in various directions. Thankfully, the lion's share darts beneath the feet of the two girls and comes to rest with a twirl and a flip. One or two continue to cartwheel about, but most drop faceup and wait quietly. The man lets out an audible "Damn!" to cover his tracks, then scoots sheepishly across the no-man's-land between himself and the teenagers. Drops to his knees in a penitent gesture, hands held palm up. The girls giggle and smile down at him, rolling their eyes with exaggeration in case any boys happen to be passing. He returns their smiles and gets down to the business of gathering up his money. The other girl, who is shorter than her compatriot and heavily freckled, points at her own mouth and mimes the word "braces." The other gal nods and smiles again, laughing into her hand.

He knows what's going on up there, the silent little game they're playing at his expense, but he is unfazed. So close to the prize now as he is. He looks up again into her eyes—his intended—and adds another smile into the mix as he reaches farther beneath her chair. One hand resting on the edge of her cushioned seat for support. He makes a meal out of this last gesture, really straining to get the maximum impact as his hand drifts over to her calf. Lands there for just an instant. Only a second, but it's enough. Oh yes. The odd thing is, what really throws him, is how she handles the situation. As his fingers trace the dimpled mountain range of her sore, drifting across the jagged flesh as it works to repair itself, there is no reaction from the young lady. Well, that's not completely true. She glances down at him—knowing full well what he's doing now—and meets his gaze dead-on. Time seems to stop for a moment, or at least to stutter along like one of those overblown special effects they use in movies these days, as they look at each other. Tick, tick, tick. He can even hear the sweep of the second hand on her Swatch as it's happening. He dares to make one last pass over the boo-boo as he snags an errant dime, then staggers to his feet and bows—a strange little gesture, to be sure—while he backs away. This time, though, only one of the girls is smiling. The tall one, the one with the wound, is just staring at him. Lips parted in a slight but obvious way. To call it inviting might be stretching it, but there's something going on between them. Man and girl. Yes, indeed. Without question.

The moment is broken only by the shrill cry of "Sweetie!" near the front doors, repeated over and over. Like the fierce screech of a tropical bird it rises, above the sound of Barry Manilow's "Mandy," which filters politely in over the public address system. In unison, the girls crane their necks in the direction of the exit to see what all the fuss is about, and the man uses this moment to retreat. He darts back behind the women's magazines and starts stumbling off toward the sound of that voice, grabbing desperately at an issue of *Popular Mechanics* as he passes. Making a beeline toward the sleepy-eyed boy at the nearest cash register. Hoping that this will be enough to cover his tracks.

Opportunity

◆

Their headlights poke through the Washington fog, picking out the ragged yellow line up ahead as it loops back and forth through various turns. The man keeps his eyes on the road; he tries the high beams but that only makes it worse. He knew that it probably would, but he gives it a go anyway. Almost immediately he returns to the standard beams and hunches forward, continuing his vigilance. The woman stares out through the windshield as well, but seems less able to concentrate on the road ahead. After a moment, she begins talking again. Not to him, exactly, but loud enough for him to hear. Certainly with enough volume for that.

". . . it's the memories that count, right? Not the actual events, I don't think, but the memories of them. What we're left with. I honestly do feel that. It's so clear to me now that we're older, well, a little older, anyway—not that we're ancient, mind you—that the moments in a life, those little situations and incidents that pile up to make it what it is, are less important, mean less to a person, than the way we remember them. Does that make any sense or am I just babbling here? 'Talking through my hat,' as my father used to call it, although I never really did understand that, that sort of phrase. Any of them, actually, from 'A stitch in time saves nine' right on down the line. But he'd say them, my father would, and you had to smile and nod and agree. That's the way it was at our place—he was the man of the house and we were there to agree with him. Not to cause a revolution. No, he 'ruled the roost,' as he liked to say. Oh yes, that he did. Well, you recall what he was like? Right, honey? I mean, he was much older when you met him—died not too long after the wedding—but you still got a sense of the man. Didn't you? I don't know that anyone who ever met him didn't get a feel for what he was like, right off. That's an admirable quality to have, I suppose. I suppose it is. To be up-front about who you are, put it out there 'right off the bat,' as he enjoyed saying—and then let people decide for themselves if they liked you or not. He was himself, through and through, right down to the end. Even to his last breath, he was his own man. 'A man's man.' You felt that, didn't you, sweetie? Sorry if I'm rambling on, but it's funny how you, when you start thinking about it, the past or whatever you'd call it—one's life—how things flood back. Like a big wave of . . . well, I don't know what. Not water, exactly, but some kind of thing. And it always happens when you're driving, have you ever noticed that? Whether it's you at the wheel, or if I'm coming home alone from a late shift, my Thursday swing shift and it's nearly midnight . . . being on the road and driving does that to me. Makes me think. I'm not completely sure that I like it. You know? That 'memory' stuff . . . well, not the memories themselves, no, of course not that—I just said that they're important, so I don't mean them— but being vulnerable, I guess, to them coming back like that. Engulfing you. That part, being at their mercy, I suppose, is what frightens me sometimes . . ."

They travel on for a while in silence. The woman drifts for a moment, remembering. Only the constant blinking of his lashes, captured by the milky light from the dashboard, betrays that the man is still awake. Watching the road. His head starts to turn but stops midway through the gesture. He reaches for a cigarette instead and, without asking, fires it up. Flicks the paper match out the slit of an open window.

"He could control us so easily, my father. All of us, right down the line, from my mother to every one of the children. Well, almost. Six older brothers and sisters and only one of them would ever think about taking him on. Verbally or otherwise. Well, of course not physically, I don't mean that—we weren't animals, raised on a farm or not. We were not savages, but I'm just saying that there was never a moment when he wasn't in complete control of us. Most all of us. He had the last word on everything, from the chores to our schoolwork to which people we dated. If we dated, that is. One of my sisters—not Lily, the oldest, not her, but the middle one, the redhead, Sarah—she was not allowed to go out with a boy until she was almost eighteen. Can you imagine? I mean, people married at that age back then; were married and had a family started by the time she was able to go off to the movies with someone. And why?—you might ask why or be thinking it there as you're driving . . . because he saw something in her, a willfulness, maybe, a sort of spirit that he felt he had to break. That's what I believe it was, personally, when I think back on it. He felt a kind of power in her that the rest of us didn't possess. A desire to be her own person, and he was not going to have any of that in his house. 'Not under my roof,' I used to hear him saying to her when they argued, out behind the barn or downstairs at night after I'd gone up to bed—I was ten years younger and so my bedtime was early in those days. The shouts of my sister and the quiet force of my father would ring out as I drifted off. It was only when she was about eighteen, as I said, that he finally allowed her any freedom in that way, to attend a film or go dancing or that type of thing. And a few months after that, of course, she was gone."

The woman glances over at her husband, but he keeps his eyes focused on the mile markers off to his right. Guiding their car through the growing mist. He tosses the butt of his Pall Mall out through the same fissure that sucked away the match. She sees this, even turns her head to watch the filter as it catches on the edge of the window before being swept away by the breeze. Moving her attention from the window to his ear before continuing.

"People would say, for a long time after that, actually, that she'd met someone in town, a soldier or the like, a traveling man, and had run off with him. Used him, really, as a ride away from us. From Father. That's what they meant when they whispered that, the people who lived in town—it was 'her way out,' they said—but that was never proved. She left no trace, you see, not really, no missing suitcase from the basement or a note or sighting of her at a gas station miles from there. She simply vanished and that was that. 'Off to the circus,' my father would say, when he finally felt like discussing it. I take that back, he never felt like discussing anything. No, by 'discussing' I simply mean that at some point—months or years later—he would mention her, Sarah, in conversation or at the dinner table and make a comment like that, one of his comments about people, and that was the only way her name was ever mentioned again. My sister."

The woman floats away again for a moment, her face upturned in the darkness. Searching for some image that seems just beyond her reach. The man drives on, eyes locked on the hood of the car.

"I once thought I saw her, in the window of a Penney's store while I was sitting in the car waiting for you . . . this flash of red passed the glass and for a moment I was sure it must be her. Over in Coeur d'Alene, of all places. I nearly got out of the car and went inside to inquire, but then you came back—I think you were picking up some caulking or something, at that hardware store over on Sherman—and before I could say anything you'd backed the car out, we still had the old Bonneville at that point, and we were off to lunch. I should've said something, I suppose, but I just didn't. I mean, when I consider it, what happened there, I know in reality it couldn't have been her, not my sister, in some department store window, but something about it, that rush of color, reminded me of her. And that, I suppose, is what I was saying before, about memory and the like. A remembered moment. How they're really so important to us, because whether it was her or not—I know, I know, how could it be?—the fact that I now have that memory is stronger and of more comfort than if I'd actually run into her there on the street. Does that make any sense, honey? What I've been saying? The pleasure that came from that one moment gave me something—truthful or not—that I might otherwise never have had. Now when I think about Sarah I remember her from the warmth of that car, me sitting inside there with the sun bouncing off the windshield, and it's a nice thing. It feels good, rather than the loss and surprise and worry that followed her disappearance all those years ago. God, I don't know if I'm making any sense out of this or not—'heads or tails,' as he used to say, my father—but it's the only way I know how to explain it. What I've been feeling as we've driven along just now . . ."

The woman steals another peek at her husband, looking for some kind of validation there. Anything. She doesn't get it, though, not yet. Rather, he adjusts the rearview mirror, trying to ward off a pair of piercing headlights that suddenly appear on the horizon behind them.

"You know, there was a time—maybe only a few weeks or so—when people began to talk. I mean, the talk about her leaving, there was a change in the mood of it. And not in any good sense of the word. 'Talk.' I mean to imply that it was gossip, horrible gossip like nothing you could imagine. We would catch snatches of it at school or church or in places like those, spots where gossip never had any business being. Yet there it was. Some folks said that she hadn't gone, had never left the farm at all but—well, I suppose there's no way around it, whom they were implicating: my father. That he had stopped my sister in some way, hurt her, even, and then hidden her somewhere out on the land because of that reckless spirit of hers. What a thing to say! Can you imagine it, even a whisper of that being said about

a family? Thankfully, I was very young and most of it never
. . . it wasn't until years later, talking to my mother as a
married woman, that I realized what had transpired that
summer. The kinds of stories that were being told. I don't
know how she made it through that, my mother, I really
don't. To lose a daughter in that way—have her run away—
and then suffer through the humiliation and pain of that
sort of speculation from your peers. Well, I can't imagine
it. But she was a strong woman, oh yes, of Norwegian heri-
tage and very practical, and somehow she put one foot in
front of the other, like she did every other day, and just
kept going. I think I have a lot of her in me, a good deal of
her, anyway. I like to think so. And whatever I am, I don't
relish the notion that I'm more like my father. No, I've
spent a lot of my life trying to distance myself from that
man and part of the effort was marrying a person who was
different as well. You, my dear, are about as different as a
man could be from him, and I love you for that. I do, I do."

A truck zips past and disappears into the murk, causing the car to shudder and swerve toward the shoulder.
The man grips the wheel and regains control. Cursing
quietly to himself. Afterward, the woman places a hand
on the man's knee and gently toys with the fabric of his
slacks. The man looks over at her for a moment, only

turning away when she smiles at him. She removes her hand slowly from his thigh, in stages.

"You have made this part of my life, this second half of it—even more, I suppose, more than that—so bearable. So wonderful, really, that it's only in moments like these, when I abandon myself to even thinking about my childhood, that it comes back to me at all. Most times, for most of this time that we have been together—in 'marital harmony,' as so many of those television folks want to call it—you have been a kind of balm against my past. You have made me happy and so, so pleased that I have the endless gift of another day with you . . ."

The man nods without taking his eyes off the interstate. There is construction up ahead and he begins the process of slowing, pumping his brakes to let the cars behind him know what's happening. The woman spots the nod and presses on, happy to finally have some reaction from her man.

"I must admit, it was not always so. No, not always. Not that I want to get into any of that, our past, but there were days in the beginning—we were so young—that I worried about what I'd done. What I might have brought on myself by marrying you. You were so quiet then, so serious, and it was hard to know what you were thinking. Feeling.

I would go around with a smile on my face, spread tightly across my lips, but all the while sensing that I might not be pleasing you in some way. In any way, for that matter. And I so wanted to do that—to please you, to know how to please a man. The cooking was there, of course, those kinds of skills I possessed from the way I grew up. Having a mother like I did and a desire, too, I think, to make the best of myself as a person. As a woman. Even when the children came, though, I thought perhaps I'd done something wrong, that I hadn't learned the recipe for making you happy. Can you imagine? That I used to lie there in our bed—remember the old bed that we bought at that garage sale, the elderly couple who was selling everything they owned, right there in their very own driveway—and worry that you didn't love me. Or worse, even like me. I guess I couldn't get a read on you—'your number'—I didn't have that in those days and I felt like I was just blundering about, wearing my housecoat and taking care of the babies but never really bringing you any kind of happiness. No kind of satisfaction beyond the common ones that a family can bring to a man. Isn't that silly? I mean, what a waste of energy. You went to work, came home at night and brought a paycheck in at the end of a month and yet there I was, so insecure that I wondered if you really loved us. Girls can be so silly, can't we? Oh yes, we're certainly capable of that. A special kind of silliness."

The first lights of the city now, Spokane in the distance. Like the fine glow of a sandy beach on a tropical night, she thinks, having seen something like it on the television. On one of the many travel shows that she watches on the weekends.

"I don't want you to worry that anything like that goes through my head any longer—it doesn't, so lose no sleep over that. It was a phase is all, a silly moment from my past that I suppose most young brides go through and I just thank the good Lord that he saw me beyond it to the other side. What nonsense!"

A long stretch of silence between them. She reaches over and touches him lightly on the trousers again, rubs his leg for a bit. Finally, he touches his fingers to hers. Holds them there for a minute before putting his hands firmly back at ten and two. The first of four exit signs zips by overhead. Liberty Lake. Otis Orchards. Green Acres will be next. Soon they will be at Opportunity and back safe. Safely to that place called home.

"I'm loathe to admit this, I really find it almost embarrassing now, but it's one of those nights when I can't stop myself so I'll just say it and be done. After my sister

left, back when those stories about her used to crop up—
I suppose I was fibbing when I said that I didn't really
understand what was happening. In actuality, I knew full
well. Yes. I was young, I'll admit that, and not all of it
made sense to me, but the idea of her leaving like that
perplexed me. Troubled me because of something that
happened. One day, maybe a week or so after Sarah was
gone, the sheriff and one of his men came out to the
house for a visit. 'A friendly visit,' he called it—he and
my father were hunting buddies and went as far back as
school together—but there was something in the air that
time that didn't seem exactly right. A look in the man's
eyes, that sheriff's, that said he was curious about all that
he'd been hearing. The way he wandered around the yard
as he spoke to my father, looking out across the fields and
toward the outbuildings, sort of scanning the horizon for
anything he didn't recognize. I was playing near the side
of the house as they talked, not really listening but near
enough to make out what was being said. And my father,
not defending himself but simply stating it, said that
he'd been with me that evening—when Sarah left. Recalled it specifically that we'd been working on a project
for my school and that's how he remembered it now,
because of helping me build a birdhouse out in his shop.

Now this was true, of course, the birdhouse that we built together—it was one of the few moments that we had as father and daughter back then—so I knew it well. When it happened. And it was not on the night of my sister's disappearance, or anywhere near it, for that matter. No, it wasn't. The sheriff, seeing me over in the grass with my dolls, looked at me without asking anything, a question of any kind, but stared into my eyes. Searching my face for the truth. I looked up at my father, and then back at the two men in uniform, and it was then when I said, in that whisper that I used to have as a child, 'Yes, that's right. My daddy and me built a birdhouse that night.' Which seemed to be enough for everyone. After they were gone, the authorities, my father came over and sat next to me—not one to ever play with toys, that man; I'm not implying that—he sat and watched me for a moment. Reached out and touched my hair with a smile and said, 'Well, well. A chip off the ol' block . . .' And you know what's funny? I might still have that thing, the project we built, out in the garage if you'd like to see it. I believe I just may do."

The right blinker begins to flash as the man works his way into the far lane. Slipping in between a Chrysler and an older Astro Van. He drifts onto the ramp and heads down toward the stoplight ahead. There is silence for a moment as the woman waits for the signal to change.

"One summer—the year before we married, in fact—I used to spend a lot of my free time off by myself. Not that I had much, what with working during the harvest and all of that, but I would wander out into the fields when I could. Searching, I suppose. Not with a shovel or anything, but just walking around, looking to see what I might notice. A rise in the dirt, a mound of some kind, whatever might spark a memory. But nothing. There was no trace of her, of that middle redheaded sister of mine, that I could find out there on our farm. No matter how hard I looked. And then we met and were married and life became quite wonderful for me. And so I rarely thought of her again until the moment outside that Penney's store in Idaho. This wondrous spark of red, so many years ago now . . ."

The car lurches forward as a green arrow appears overhead. It darts around a slow-moving Honda and disappears into the haze of the underpass. The taillights, like the flaming eyes of a storybook monster, become smaller and smaller and smaller still. And then they are gone, swallowed up by the endless dark of an infinite night.

Spring Break

◈

He looks at the tears in her eyes and thinks twice about proceeding. Well, not twice, really, not like in the sense that he isn't going to go through with it—the breakup, I mean—but imagines that they can maybe wait for a moment. Get their bearings. Regroup. Then he figures, Screw it, let's get this done, I've got class, and pushes on. It's not that he doesn't care about her, not exactly, anyway, but just that he's in a hurry. His 1:30 tutorial is way across campus and on a good day he practically has to run to get there on time. And this is definitely not that. A good day. No way is this one going into the pantheon of very fine days that he's set aside for himself. This is not even close.

It starts with the "we need to talk" call he barely catches in the bathroom when he switches his cell on, just to check the messages. Seven A.M. and she's already calling the house. What if he'd accidentally left the phone on and that had happened in the breakfast nook or as he was sitting down to watch *Good Morning America* for ten minutes with the family? Not good, that's what that is. No way you get out of explaining a 7 A.M. call to your cell phone, I don't care who you are. One of those takes plenty of explaining. Plenty.

"Yeah, yeah, I'll be there, I promise," he whispers into the receiver over the protective hiss of his shower water. "I will! Jesus, I said, 'I promise,' OK?" He hangs up and slips the Motorola deep into his bathrobe pocket for safekeeping as he starts to peel off his Jockeys. He glances in the mirror, mercifully frosting over now, and promises a day or two at the gym this week. And if not this week then definitely the next, since break will be starting up and he'll have a little more time to himself. A lot more, actually, if he can get her off his back for five minutes. He knows that only a breakup—I mean, a complete severing of their relationship—can make that happen, and he begins to steel himself to the idea as he steps into the steamy glass box before him. He taps himself on the head, muttering, "Dumbshit!" under his breath, and returns to the robe. Switches off the phone. Jumps back into the shower.

Hustling up the long stairway that leads from the faculty parking lot to the main campus, he has a moment for reflection. Hair still damp, he begins to think—which is pretty dangerous at the best of times. Before a breakup, it's practically a death wish. Thinking is overrated, anyway, he philosophizes as he lumbers up the stairs, pausing halfway for a breather. A freshman, maybe a sophomore—it's definitely the backside of an undertwenty—dashes past and continues the ascent. Probably doesn't have a sticker, he imagines, consoling himself with this notion between breaths. Couldn't afford it, so she's gotta park in the outer lots. This makes him feel better about himself, his station in life, if only briefly. He turns now, readying himself for the final push to the summit, all the while wondering who the genius was who decided to put such a steep set of stairs next to the faculty parking area. "A woman," he mutters aloud, trying to take the last two steps simultaneously. He just catches the edge of his left Rockport on the granite lip of the landing and goes down hard. On one knee. Assessing the damage, he spots a tiny tear in his Dockers—

hardly noticeable, but it's going to bug him for the rest of the day. "Definitely some woman architect . . ." he says absently, not to anyone in particular but just as a statement of fact. He remembers reading it somewhere. In one of those crappy color brochures he'd received in his welcome packet, maybe. Women, for the most part, designed the whole college, and now it seems as though he's the one who's going to have to pay for it.

A glance at his Fossil tells him he's still got an hour before the fateful showdown. Or encounter. He prefers this to "showdown," with its relatively bad connotations of a hail of bullets and someone being buried in an unmarked grave. A someone who looks remarkably like himself. Yes, better to think of it as simply an encounter. A meeting between two modern, savvy, educated people. He smiles at this, imagining that some good might actually come out of the meeting. He checks his watch again, remembering that she isn't free until 12:30, what with her karate class and all. Well, its self-defense, to be fair, but all that stuff is some sort of karate. That's how he sees it, anyway. "It's all Asian and it's all beyond me," he'd said at dinner one time, causing a silence to slip over the entrée like a fog bank. He'd actually watched her once, back when he'd been obsessed with her—or *liked* her, at least. Sneaked down to the field house where her class was and sat in the stands, studying her. The way her perfect little body moved, that tilt of her head as she performed a throw or moved into a stance. His mind started to drift—no cause for alarm, this often happened—and he could easily imagine himself at the mercy of one of those tosses. Some sort of argument about girls and parties or whatever and there he'd be, cartwheeling through the air, end over end, past the art deco lamp that she loves, and down onto her glass coffee table. Crash! With her temper—redheads are famous for that—this was not out of the realm of possibility. Not even out of the fiefdom. It could happen. He had shuddered at the thought, then slipped back out of the auditorium without her knowing.

If he was honest with himself—which he rarely felt much if any compulsion to be—he'd been thinking about this breakup for a while now. Planned it out in his head like a Peckinpah action sequence. Maybe it was the karate class she was in, but the idea of breaking up with her always came with images of shattering glass and spurting blood. All in slow motion. Even horses, which made no real sense but helped complete the analogy. And there was nothing he disliked more than some cheap, aborted analogy. Bad analogies sucked, as far as he was concerned.

He bides some of the remaining time watching coeds. Not any that he would be interested in—rebounding is difficult and can easily be messed up. It's very simple to jump too fast, too far, and end up in the same snake pit as before. Girls are tricky, he reasons, content for the moment to simply look. Watch. Imagine. He prides himself on being great at imagining. Several cuties wander past, giggling and fairly intent on wasting their parents' money. Two or three catch his eye, throw him a smile. One he sort of knows, a little, from last semester. They might have even gone out once or hooked up at some postfinals blow-out. It's hard to recall with girls like that. The Gap-clad, Abercrombie-assed, ponytailed masses get harder and harder to differentiate the longer he's at this place. So, he decides to do what he always does. Smile back. Something about her, a brushing of her bangs as she passes, suggests that they've slept together, but he has no hard evidence to support this. He'd have to see her naked to be sure, and there is no chance of that right now, of this he is quite certain. See, he never forgets a body. Not ever. And in his own humble way, he prides himself on this. Every foot, elbow, curve of the neck is catalogued somewhere in that head of his. Why do they care so much if we can recall a birthday or some damn anniversary, he wonders, when it's so much more caring to make note of the length of her calves, the bridge of her nose. An imperfection that dances in her left pupil. All this is important. The rest is artifice.

It's edging toward 12:45 when he spots her making a move through the library crowd. Her precise haircut cutting this way and that as she moves to the reading lounge. He has absently picked up a copy of *Bazaar* but discards it now, knowing how she hates it when he tears out the photos. Not to pin on his office wall or anything silly like that, but just to consider in private. An attractive girl, one who has managed to get herself in *Bazaar*, anyway, is always worth a second glance.

She sits on the black vinyl chair next to him, a fake Barcelona, with an easy, inscrutable grace—thanks to the karate training, he reasons—and looks at him. Make that *stares*. Not a word out of her, just the death stare. Like that one tractor beam thingy in *Star Wars*. Locked on him and ready to do some damage. One hand twitching. Probably deciding which punch to throw first. Maybe rip his heart out and show it to him before he dies—that old Bruce Lee classic. He sits back on his cushioned love seat a bit, hopefully just out of her range, and decides to pitch right in. And then it happens. The crying starts up. He's got to give her some credit here, because this is pretty smooth, this tactic. He hadn't even come up with a game plan for this one. Nope. He'd run the shouting-match–fisticuffs–chase-across-campus scenario through his head a dozen times, but this middlebrow, mascara-running, silent plea for sympathy hadn't even seemed like a remote possibility.

"Look, I could say a bunch of stuff, really, all kinds of pretty standard guy crap that you'd see right through and none of it would make this any easier, so I might as well just say it. OK?" He checks to see how that worked, whether it appears to have any lasting effect. She remains quiet, though, like some Jazz Age painting—it's her bobbed hairdo that brings this to mind—simply looking back at him. Silent.

"I really like what we had, you know, all those din-ners and movies at your place. You're great, you *totally* are, and I loved being in class with you. I learned a ton, honestly. You're awesome with Shakespeare . . . *Tam-ing of the Shrew* really came alive for me. But . . . I just don't dig this anymore, all right? I mean, not so much." Nothing from her. A couple more tears, but they're starting to mean less and less now that he's waist-deep in them.

"I just feel like we were becoming too serious, and people are, like, you know, getting suspicious. Yeah. I even had a few guys ask me about it. My parents, too, and I know I shouldn't be living with 'em and whatnot, I know that, but that's a whole other issue. Look, bottom line is I'm twenty-three and you're the head of my department. My dad even works for you! That's heavy, when you think about it. It really is. I also . . . no offense, but I think you're sort of a mother figure for me, and that's starting to freak me out. It was cool at first—not that my mom has a body like yours or anything—but it's getting so I can't see the 'real' you because of it." OK, time to wrap it up now. He's spinning his wheels, he can feel it, and he needs to just introduce a strong finish here and be done with this nonsense. "I guess . . . I guess, overall, I just don't really like you that much. Not enough, anyhow. I mean, I like you, I'll always *like* you, but . . ."

He flinches as she stands because she may be assuming an attack position. His hands start to involuntarily move—just to protect the face—when he realizes that she is only grabbing at her purse, rising up to smooth out her skirt. She doesn't say a word as she turns and starts off. "Well, hey, that wasn't so bad," he whispers, congratulating himself on the overall ease of the operation. But it's not over yet. He should've known better than that. She pivots in the foyer, about thirty yards away, and stares back at him. Just stares. Burning twin holes through the front of his Old Navy sweater. A minute goes by. Maybe two. Then, out of nowhere, she lashes out with one foot at a wooden book-return cart. Ninja-like. Her loafer makes contact and the rolling shelf careens across the marble, smacking a pillar and spilling copies of *National Geographic* across the floor. A few paperbacks. She misses most of this, however, having turned away on impact—she is more intent on quickly making her way out through the security doors. The last he sees of her is that haircut zipping past the undergrads on her way to the English Department. "Geez, she's crazy." He consoles himself with this as he stands, faking a yawn. As an afterthought, he reaches down and tears the cover from the *Bazaar* magazine. Shoves it down into his cargo pants as he heads off in the opposite direction. Toward his tutorial. Toward spring break. Toward freedom.

Wait

◈

Wait. Wait, I tell myself. No need to rush. Wait for it. If I can. I will if I can. I'm trying. I swear, I'm trying, but the thought of her. It's hard. So hard. So I close my eyes. Concentrate. Thinking of her. The smell of her, that's first. I always smell her first. Fresh, glorious, lovely. And hovering there. A foot away. Maybe less, but seemingly a foot. Close enough to touch. Yes, to touch if I wanted. And I want to. But I won't. Not yet. Wait. Wait, I tell myself. How long have I waited like this? Before? I can't count the times. No, I can't, don't want to. It's frightening. To wait. But I do.

What if she denies me, smiles and moves off? She could, she might. Would she? Hasn't before but that means nothing. She could easily turn. Away. Against. And I'd be lost. I would. To not have her, have that, I'd be lost. Left there, blinking, the half-light of pulled blinds and expectation. Patterned tie askew and lost. So I wait. Wait, I tell myself. As she inches closer. Not far now, not far at all. But holding off. Teasing. Did I say something? At dinner? A harsh remark, a misread glance? I play it back, all of it. Scan the menu of our conversation for an oversight, a cigarette not lit quickly enough. Have I failed? I hope not, not now. So close. A breath away. But nothing. I remember nothing but this moment. This waiting. Rain on the window and waiting. She's like that, though; I calm myself. One week difficult, the next rewarding. It's a game, this wondering. What'll it be this time? All week, at my desk, the washroom, the conference area that looks out on the lake. Each day, I play it out, pondering. How did it go? How will it be? Does she love me? Could she? Yes? But nothing. Not a sign from above, from her. Nothing. An inch closer, perhaps. But nothing yet. So I wait. Wait, I tell myself. She's here, it's coming. Just wait.

It used to be anywhere, any spot she wanted. My apartment, her choice. She would point and in we'd go.

Without speaking. Up to her. The control. But it's different now, a tighter focus. Always the same. The kids' room. A turquoise throw. Gift from Christmas. That's the spot. Dangerous. But I lie there, waiting. Wait. Wait, I tell myself. Brooks Brothers shirt untucked and waiting. For her. And still she lingers. Getting close now. Time for Scouts to finish, wife's late night at the office, people arriving back. Back home. Risky. For fifty dollars a week, a ring from the bellman. Push the envelope, she says. Count to twenty after the buzz. See if we can make it. Try to bargain, beg sometimes. She's having none of it. Not today. An inch closer. And then I smell her again. Always smell her first. And so I wait. Wait, I tell myself. Go to church; I sit and wait. A business lunch; I wait. Through Peter Jennings and *Friends* and an infomercial I've learned to wait. For next Tuesday. Each Tuesday. So I can wait. Oh yes. Because she's here. Almost ready. She hovers there, reading book titles off a little wicker shelf. She's read that one. And that. And that one, too. When she was a babysitter. And as a child. I flame at this, not embarrassed but aware. Past embarrassed. Beyond it. Well beyond. But aware. Of everything. Me. Her. Our arrangement. Our ages. And lives. And wants. I know not to move, to fidget, to ask. Ask nothing, she says. Just wait. Wait, I tell myself. Study, yearn, desire. These are fine. Allowed. But not the rest. Not yet. No, I must wait. So I do. I wait. And wait. And wait. And then a burst, static. Loud. A sign from below. She smiles. I smile. Lips part. To greet. To welcome. To invite. I am hers . . .

The young woman leans into it as she pisses, grimacing, covering him. Carefully missing the rug. A two-fingered kiss and she is gone. Counting cash. He lies there, hearing the elevator approach but unable to move.

Layover

◆

Now there's a nice lay, he thinks to himself, as he politely sidesteps and lets her out of line so she can carry her food over to the condiment island. A flicker of a smile on her lips as she passes. A flicker, nothing more, but it's there. He hurriedly pays for his order, not waiting for the $1.84 in change or the receipt. No time for that now. She'd smiled at him. He juggles his two trays, weaving his way through the airport crowd as he prays for an opening near her, by the ketchup pump or the napkin dispenser, at the very least. The napkins would be a stretch, but he could manage it. He'll force his way in if he has to. He promises himself this. Well, maybe not force, but he'll definitely say, "Excuse me," pointedly. Definitely. She isn't going to get away that easily, not after a smile. No way.

"Could you pass me a spork?" she asks, trying to keep her burger together with a free hand. Looking right at him. She could have picked anyone, but she's looking right into his eyes.

Like clockwork, he mentally notes as he picks up an individually wrapped utensil and hands it over. A finger brushing hers. The slightest of intimacies, but at the moment of impact it feels as if a chorus of angels has burst into song. That might be going a little far, but it seems very similar to that. It does. People are beginning to pile up behind him, and he grabs a packet of relish for emphasis as he offers, "I hate that name, don't you? Did they have to call it 'spork'? I mean, why not a 'foon' or something equally stupid?"

"Yeah, I know." She flashes a grin while sneaking a couple of fries.

"So . . . you stuck here, too?" he ventures, filling a few paper thimbles with mustard as cover while he engages.

"Yep," she mumbles, more to herself than anything, but it allows him to lean in a bit closer. The ol' lean-in, a classic.

"Sorry? I couldn't hear you—that announcement," he shouts, pointing up at the ceiling with an elbow as he says it. Another smile floats his way. Jesus, he thinks, what a pushover. She would do me right here, or in the lounge, at least, a hand job under my coat or something. No question.

"I never get a call on the courtesy phone," she says, laughing. Not a giggle, mind you, this is a full-bodied laugh. "Not once in my adult life have I ever been called to that damned white phone! Guess I'm not very special." And she holds eye contact the whole time. Bingo. She takes a nugget from his conversation and personalizes it. Adds a little melodramatic flourish at the end. Perfect response. Perfect.

Why not just press a handwritten note into my palm and be done with it? A pair of panties slipped into my carry-on? She is begging for it, he imagines as he gives that faux chuckle of his, the good one that most everyone at the office likes and chuckles along with. "Well, let me be the first," he suggests. "You go stand over there near the receiver and I'll have them page you with a desperate message or something." That could've been better, a stronger joke at the end or maybe a wink thrown in, but it seems to work.

"And what would the desperate message be? Huh?" Complete amusement on her part now. Absolutely complete.

"Oh, I'd think of something." He chuckles again (risky to use it twice in the same conversation, but so far so good). A bull's-eye. She looks up expectantly while blowing a stray piece of auburn hair out of her eyes. Waits another second. People are grabbing things from around them now, realizing that a "moment" is officially taking place here.

"Come on, don't keep me in suspense. Tell me what it would be."

"Umm . . . something like, I dunno, maybe like 'Hey, tell the redhead that I'm nuts about her and to get home safely, because I already miss her.' Something like that," he says without even looking over. He doesn't need to. That was a cruise missile, that one. If she were an Iraqi, she'd be dead now. He gives it another beat, throws some straws down near the three corn dogs, then glances over. She's still staring at him.

"That's the nicest thing anyone's said to me in six years," she whispers. "Seriously, since I graduated, that's the best line I've heard." It's not a tear, but something's definitely going on in those blue, blue eyes of hers. Liquid of some sort.

"Then you're welcome, and it's not a line. You deserve to hear it every day. Twice," he says, chuckling one last time. A new personal best. Three chuckles, and not a sliver of suspicion out of her. Excellent. He realizes it's time to make a move, see what happens. Test the theory. One last smile on his part, what the hell, he even tosses in the wink, and then he turns to go. At the last possible second, it happens. Her voice lifts, up over the throb of the crowd.

"Listen . . . you wanna sit together or something?"

To turn quickly would be wrong—too desperate, he figures. Better to stop slowly, maybe sigh or something, with a slight but perceptible drop of the shoulders, and then gracefully look back. A weary frown.

"Geez, you know what, I'd love to, but . . ."

"You can't, no, I understand . . ."

"It's just, I'm with some colleagues," he finally offers. "I've got their stuff here, and they're way down by D23."

"No problem," she says bravely, but she is clearly disappointed. Clearly. He lets the moment hang between them, lets her dance on the gallows of expectation a bit longer, then bequeaths her another look. The "if only" look that has carried him from junior high to this very minute, standing here before her.

"Just my luck," he says. A thin smile and shrug from her. He fires one back, matching her shrug for shrug. He has to fire one back; it's expected. Then one step each. Maybe two. He counts out "one, two, three, four, five" to himself, even using "Mississippi" in between, before pivoting around. Checking again. And she's still looking. Checkmate. Bobby Fischer would come out of hiding to watch him work, days like these. Before he can fully savor the victory, however, the floating sound of the courtesy phone erupts overhead, raining down with cleansing static. Big smiles from both of them on that one, the timing impeccable. Courtesy *ex machina*. And exit, stage left.

He snaps open the Money section of *USA Today* for emphasis, shuffles the pages a bit, just to let the girls know he's reading, to take it a little easy with the Hello Kitty chatter. Doesn't even glance up at the wife. The food was a touch cold on delivery, but he felt he needed to stop for the paper after that. The "interlude." Something to read, a helpful moat between him and the family. It had taken a minute to find them, the girls having got it into their collective heads to snag a corner table instead of the perfectly good one he'd selected. Doesn't matter. Whatever keeps them quiet. He scans the stocks one last time—doesn't own any but enjoys seeing who's losing out—then folds the paper once, and over again. In the distance, a flash of red. He looks up, cautiously now; wives have radar. And there she is, the condiment gal. Sixty feet away. A whole booth to herself, busiest airport in the world, and she scores a booth. Staring straight at him. Another one of those looks, but with a twist this time. The mouth a bit turned down, the eyes a touch narrower. There could be disgust there; he's not absolutely sure. It's hard at twenty yards to read disgust with certainty. Might be the burger not agreeing with her, but probably not. She even shakes her head a touch when one of the girls erupts on his side, up from under the table and suddenly at his throat, pawing him, tugging on his ear. He silently tries to explain, plead his case, prove that he's different. That he'd give it all up for her, if only. If only. He looks over again, but she has vanished. Left her tray and faded into the lunch crowd. Maybe never even really existed. He wonders about this as he toys with his girl's braids. Adjusts her tiny sweater. Brushes crumbs from her flushed, tired cheeks.

"You have beautiful children," comes the voice, not three feet away. He hadn't planned on this one. The surprise attack. Out of the jungle at dawn. The girls titter and make faces, his spouse wipes ketchup from her chin and grins up foolishly, he buries a "Thank you" into his Sprite. He considers using the chuckle a fourth time but immediately backs away from the idea.

"You must be so proud," she says, holding this a touch too long. Nearly an inappropriate amount of time, he feels, with no clear response from their side of the table. Finally, she moves off, her loafers making a soulful squeak as she treads along the rubberized Spanish-tile floor. A carry-on rattling behind her. A blast of white noise from the courtesy phone covering her tracks.

"That was sweet," says the wife, breaking the latest détente. One of her hopeful looks.

"Yeah," he states, flatly. Directly. Scooping up the Life section and burrowing in. Thinking all the while, She wants me. She wants me. I know she wants me.

A Second of Pleasure

◈

". . . all right, here's the thing."

"What?"

"The thing of it is, I don't really want to go. I don't. I guess that would be the actual thing of it."

"Oh."

"Yeah."

"I see."

"I know I'm standing here, and I've got my bag in my hand and all that, but if you were to ask me right now, 'Hey, do you really wanna do this, go to the country this weekend?' I'd say, 'No, not really.' I would, I'd say, 'No thank you. I don't.'"

"But . . . you already said yes before. I mean, before now. Today. This minute. You said yes earlier this week."

"I know I did, you're right, I did do that."

"And that was, like, Tuesday or something."

"Late Tuesday, I think, but yeah. Yes, it was."

"So, I mean, you . . . you had all week to say something."

"I know, I know that, and I should've, but . . ."

"The train's out of here in, like, ten minutes . . ."

"I realize this is sudden. I mean, unexpected."

"Very. It's very much that . . ."

"I know. I didn't want to do this . . . I mean, I did, I did want to tell you earlier, call you or something, because, believe me, it would've been easier that way. On the phone or in an e-mail to the office, but I really was on the fence here. I couldn't decide. I'd felt this general sense for a while, I mean, this week—don't know how long exactly—but then today I had this . . . a thing happen. This idea that I should say something."

"So . . . you gave it a lot of thought, then?"

"Huh?"

"I mean, it didn't . . . the idea didn't just pop into your head this minute. Standing here under the clock or whatever. You've mulled it over."

"Yes. A bit."

"Considered it all . . ."

"Well, I didn't . . . you know, I wasn't up at night because of it, but, yeah. I tried to find the right approach to . . . but then I'm suddenly standing here and we're buying snacks and I'm thinking, Gosh, I need to say something. I need to, and I have to do it now. That's what I was doing a moment ago, when you touched my shoulder and said, 'You OK?' That's what I was doing at that very moment."

"All right."

"I was coming to a decision about it."

"Without me."

"I'm sorry?"

"I'm saying that you were deciding about our weekend by yourself. The fate of it. Without any input from me."

"Well, sort of . . . yes."

"Got it."

"I said already that I should've mentioned something sooner . . ."

"Yes, but I think you meant that you should've come up with the answer quicker, made a move about this before now . . . but not that I ever needed to be included in any of it."

"Umm, no, I just meant that I . . ."

"That's how it came off. When you said that, just now, that's what it sounded like."

"Okay. Sorry. What I meant was . . ."

"No, I get it. I see what you're saying . . ."

"It's not like I was purposely trying to leave you out, it's just that, you know, when you're trying to figure a thing through, a thing like this . . . it's sort of a one-sided deal, that's all. Right?"

"I wouldn't know."

"Come on . . ."

"No, I wouldn't. Seriously. I'm big on sharing. On being open about stuff, whether it's painful stuff or not."

"Oh, please."

"I am. I'm completely that way."

"Fine, I understand."

"No, I don't think you do. You don't or you wouldn't approach this in so cavalier a manner. My feelings."

"I'm not being . . ."

"You're riding all over them, absolutely you are. This minute. Like one of the Seventh Cavalry or something. It couldn't be worse if I was some Sioux squaw, running along the riverbank with a baby in my arms, trying not to get shot in the back. I mean it . . ."

"That's a little dramatic, isn't it?"

"I think it's a pretty suitable metaphor . . ."

"Well, it's a bit much, I think. Plus, you couldn't really . . . I mean, you're a man. It doesn't even really work, your analogy."

"I know that, I know. But you get my point . . ."

"I do, yes, but it's . . . it just seems kind of grand, that's all."

"You think?"

"Sort of."

"I'm hurt, so I lashed out. Sorry."

"No, I understand, I'm just saying . . . look, isn't it better that I bring this up now than in the middle of dinner tonight, or tomorrow during a second set of tennis or something? I am trying to be fair to both of us . . ."

"I see. This is you being 'fair.'"

"Well, in a way, yes. Trying to, anyhow."

"Great."

"I really am trying to be . . ."

"Terrific."

"See, now you're just angry. Getting all huffy and everything."

"No, I'm not. I'm really not."

"Sounds like it to me."

"I'm not. I'm just taking it all in. Dealing with it . . . as our train's leaving."

"It's not going yet, we've still got a few minutes."

"Whatever. Doesn't really matter, now, does it? It's moot."

"Is it?"

"I think so. I think it was invented for moments like this, that word. 'Moot' times just like this one."

"I don't know. What I'm saying is there's still time. Whether we both go, or just you, there's still time to get on board."

"That's comforting . . ."

"Look, I don't want this turning into some 'thing' here, standing out where anyone can see us, I really don't. I'm telling you how I feel and I'm sorry if it hurts or you don't like it. I can't help it, I needed to say what I'm feeling."

"And you did."

"Yes, I did do that and I'm glad. Now we should probably . . ."

"What?"

"I don't know, it's just an expression. Well, not an 'expression,' exactly, but me trying to get the conversation going again. Started in some other direction."

"Started?"

"Moving, then. However you want to look at it. I was trying to move things along in a positive direction. If I'm not going, then we should cash in my ticket, you should get down to the platform, that sort of deal."

"Wow, you've got an answer for everything today. That's great . . ."

"I'm just being practical. No reason you shouldn't enjoy the weekend, I just don't feel like it this time. I don't, so I'm letting you know that, up front."

"Well, not exactly 'up front.' No, that would've been Tuesday night, up front. Wednesday morning at the latest."

"Right, yes, that's true . . ."

"No, I think you'd have to go ahead and call this 'last minute.' What you're doing here. Besides thoughtless and shitty and maybe even mean-spirited . . . I think this would go down as 'last minute.'"

"I deserve that, so go ahead . . ."

"I don't know if you do or not—deserve it—it's just how this makes me feel."

"I don't think I should be taken to task for being honest . . ."

"No?"

"No, I really don't."

"Yeah, but I don't get why. You keep saying that, that you don't want to go and you have your little ideas about how we should proceed and whatnot, but you haven't said why you're . . ."

"Because I feel bad for him."

"Oh."

"That's why. OK?"

"You feel bad."

"Yes, I do."

"For him? You mean *him* him?"

"Yes. My husband."

"Got it."

"See? And I don't think that's any way to slip away and start a weekend together, some illicit weekend with another person, by feeling all guilty about your spouse."

"No, I . . . I suppose I agree. That's . . . damn."

"Yes. I feel the same way. 'Damn.' I didn't mean for this to happen."

"I'm sure you didn't, but . . ."

"I was packing when it started. Going up and down-stairs and throwing a suitcase together, having already laid the groundwork—heading off to the Cape with some friends, getaway with the girls, blah-blah-blah—and I saw him, sitting in the kitchen in his suit, still in his suit jacket from work and having cereal for dinner. He was eating cereal and reading the back of the box. It was a kid's cereal and it had a few little games on it, like a word-find and one of those mazes that children do while they're wait-ing to eat, and he was there at our breakfast table near the window seat, and he was doing it. I mean, tracing his finger along the maze and trying to find his way out, and it struck me. It did. Right then it kind of hit me like a static shock or something, a little bolt of heat lightning. I sat down right there on the stairs and couldn't breathe for a minute, watching him. Leaning forward with his tie hanging in the bowl, almost touching the milk, as he worked at getting to the other side of that little jumble of lines. And I realized that I was feeling something that I hadn't felt in a long time. Something for him. My hus-band. These . . . emotions."

"My. My oh my."

"Yes, I know."

"That is a surprise . . ."

"Believe me, for me, too."

"I'm sure."

"I mean, we've done this before. You know? Done it and I didn't think twice about it, about what it all meant or how he might feel. No, I just did it. But not today . . . and so I came down here, I mean, brought my bag and everything, got here on time, but ever since then I've been feeling it. This sensation of doing something wrong. Bad. And maybe that's what I'd been feeling all week, some form of this but not able to put a name to it, my finger on it. Maybe that was it."

"So, what you're saying is, you can't go. Don't want to."

"No, I don't. Not this weekend, anyway."

"Not ever, maybe, from what I'm hearing."

"I'm not sure. Honestly, I don't really . . . I'm confused by it myself."

"Right."

"I am. I hope you believe me because I truly am torn up about it."

"No, I believe you. I do. I'm looking at you and I can see that, feel that you're telling me the truth. It's not just some line."

"Absolutely not."

"And I appreciate that. Would've been nice if you could've put your finger on it, like, say, Thursday or something, but . . ."

"I did want to warn you, I mean, that I had this nagging thing going on, but . . ."

"The hotel's booked now and everything . . ."

"I know. I can pay you for it, half, I'm saying, if that helps at all, or . . ."

"No, come on, please, you know it's not about that. The cost. I'm just saying that it's a shame, some beautiful room overlooking the water standing empty this weekend because we didn't get it together . . . that's all. It bothers me somehow."

"It was just the image of him, sitting there in the breakfast nook with that carton of Count Chocula, that did me in. I saw him with a puddle of brown milk in his bowl and it all made sense to me, what I'd been doing to him. The hurt that was piling up because of this. Us."

"*Us?* You mean like *us* us?"

"Yes. You and me."

"So, is that how you think of us? In terms of hurt?"

"In some way, yes. I mean, I've loved it when we've been together—at our best it's breathtaking and exciting and, well, so many things. Like indoor fireworks. I've felt all this, just . . . stuff with you that I haven't felt for the longest time, but . . ."

"What? What is it?"

"As I sat there watching him eat, trying to scoop up those last little marshmallow pieces with his spoon and make his way out of that puzzle, I felt some kind of pleasure. Only a second, really, but it was so deep and so honest, and it was in that instant that I remembered everything about why we had come together and married and had children and had lasted this long. Through sickness and money troubles and recessions and a war and even you and me. We had weathered all of that and were still together—that man in there and myself—because of a kind of pleasure we brought to one another, something that . . . if I'm honest about it . . . you and I will probably never have a chance of finding."

"Jesus, that's . . ."

"I'm just being honest."

"Yes. Brutally honest."

"I'm sorry."

"You could've . . . I mean, you could just say, 'I can't make it this weekend.' You don't have to drive a stake through the heart of it, do you?"

"I don't know. Maybe. Yes, maybe I do."

"Jesus. That's . . . shit."

"I wish I had a picture that I could show you of the moment I witnessed there. That second of pleasure. I think then you'd understand."

"I don't mean to be blunt or anything, but honestly . . . I doubt it."

"Maybe you're right."

"I think you're just feeling guilty."

"Yeah, that might be it, too. God, I don't know . . ."

"And if that's the case, then OK. I understand that, hell, I feel the same thing. Every time I look at one of my kids and say how bad I feel about missing a soccer game or that kind of thing—I don't really, I could care less about that crap, I hate soccer, actually, but I detest lying to them. The act of it."

"No, I agree. I've always disliked that part of this."

"Not so much with my wife, because, well, I'm not sure. She's an adult, I suppose, and can fend for herself, or maybe I'm just so used to it, after doing it so often over so many years that it's actually become not just natural but kind of comforting, in a way. It warms me a bit, to look into her eyes and deceive her."

"Oh. Well, I hope that's not true . . ."

"That sounds bad. No, I don't mean that I relish it or look for opportunities to do it, of course not. It's just that it's become a kind of ritual between us, even if she's not really in on it. It's a form of closeness, actually. I mean, I wouldn't lie to just anybody. I guess that's what I'm saying . . ."

"I think I understand."

"Good. I'm not sure I even mean it, I'm just speaking off-the-cuff. You've got me all flustered here, what with the . . ."

"I know."

"So, forgive me."

"No need. I just . . . we sort of got off the track here, but you see what I'm saying. Why I had to say something."

"I guess I do. Yes."

"So . . ."

". . . yeah. So."

"I should probably get back."

"All right."

"And you? Are you going to . . . ?"

"I think I'll still head up. I mean, I've done all the legwork here, might as well enjoy it. I can probably get some work done, maybe a round of golf or something. Or else I'll come back early, take the kids to a movie."

"That'd be nice. Weather's supposed to hold through Sunday."

"That's good."

"I hope the hotel's nice. It sounded lovely . . ."

"Yeah, should be. I'll cancel your treatments, at the spa there."

"You sure? I can call if you . . ."

"No, no problem. I'll take care of it."

"Fine then. So, I guess I'll see you . . ."

"When?"

"Oh, umm . . . I don't know, actually. I just said that. It's one of those things you say when you're not sure what else to say. It's filler."

"Right."

"I don't know if we will. Or should, even. Not for a while."

"Figured as much."

"Yes. I mean, the way I'm feeling . . ."

"Uh-huh."

"I think they just called for . . ."

"Yeah, I better get down there. What was it again?"

"Track Twenty-three."

"Yep, that's it. OK, so . . ."

"Take care."

". . . lemme just ask you something, quick, and you can be honest. It seems like it's time for that right now, honesty, so go ahead. Be honest."

"All right. If I can."

"Did you, in all these months, did you ever feel that thing for me, what you just described about the cereal and your husband sitting there?"

"Well . . ."

"I'm not saying that exact same kind of 'pleasure,' but something. Anything. From what I ever did, or us together? Did you?"

". . . ummm . . ."

"You can tell me. It's OK, I'm just curious."

"No, I didn't. No. Not ever."

"All right. I was just wondering."

"I'm sorry."

"No problem. It's . . . I'll see you, then."

"Yes. Sometime."

"Bye."

"Good-bye."

Look at Her

◆

Look at her. Seriously, look. There she is, over there. Unbelievable, right? I mean, I can't take my eyes off her. Really, I can't. I've been standing here next to the sliding glass door all night and just watching her. The way she shifts her weight from foot to foot as she studies people, her little sigh that seems to wait until everyone has stopped speaking and then just pokes out above the silence. Everything. Wait, there, did you see that? See how she follows a person around the room with her eyes, sizing them up, whispering to herself the whole time? I love that. She did that to me about an hour ago, the watching-judging-mumbling thing, and I had to step outside a minute, grab some fresh air. I'm telling you, she's got it going on, you know what I mean? She does. I don't know what "it" is or how you get it, but I know it when I see it. That head-turning, mind-blowing gift from the heavens that makes a woman who she was, is, and has the potential to become. This lady has it in spades, and I'm standing here holding a soft drink, all but speechless. She's amazing.

And nobody's looking at her, that's what I can't believe. They're not. Most of the guys here, studio animals who band together like a bunch of nomads, are standing around and chatting up some golden-haired starlet with a white jacket and a smile, and that's fine. Totally cool. Whatever makes you happy, right? She's the obvious one, anyway, I mean, when you look around the room, take all the women in with the quick glance, she'd be the one that you might first be drawn to. The body. And the face. Fashionable slacks and purse. That flash of expensive white inside her mouth. The teeth *are* nice, I'll give her that. You have teeth like that, you're halfway home in this town. But the other woman, the one I've been following with my eyes—over there by the sushi tray now and taking drink orders from industry types who don't seem to see her because she's married and over forty and isn't wearing anything leather—has a different sort of deal working for her. A kind of pouty-lip mystique that reminds me of Jeanne Moreau. The way she was in that film; you know, the one that broke her out big; *The Lovers,* I think it was. See, Jeanne's the wife of some newspaper guy, and she drifts into an affair or two. Wearing these big floral print dresses and that look in her eyes. Well, this woman I'm watching here has that same type of thing happening for her. That thing that says, "As a matter of fact, yes, I *am* a woman, what's it to you?" And that's why I keep staring at her.

She must be the wife of the production VP who's throwing this little party in the hills, I'm not sure. I don't think she's a guest, at least doesn't seem to be. No one's talking to her. She's got a cocktail dress on and that tiny pearl necklace and that's about it. One eye that she keeps rubbing behind her glasses. Her shoes came off long ago, so I'm guessing she lives here. Just guessing, but I'm pretty sure by now. What is it about her? I wonder. I mean, there's a bunch of women here my age, at least ten. Blondes, a redhead or two (which I completely dig), even a couple college girls. Don't really know what they're doing here, but they make it nice. Like a school dance or something. And each one, these other women, I mean, has qualities about her that I would normally find captivating. At least worth hitting on, if we were on a plane together or whatever. That one over there, with the green turtleneck and the scarf, what's her story? I mean, it's the middle of August and she's sporting that big wool wrap around her neck, which is totally out of place and, therefore, pretty damn sexy. And the girl with the Bennington T-shirt, very nice. Any woman with something to read on her clothes is sending you an open invitation, in my book. Normally I'd shoot over there and size her up, make a lame comment about the college or something, get a number, you know. The usual. But not tonight.

Tonight it's just me and that lady over there with the black dress in all her middle-aged glory. I should go say something to her. I really should, because you let a moment of this magnitude go and you're gonna stumble around like some lost soul the rest of your days, muttering to yourself about the one that got away. Or like that guy in *Citizen Kane*—the funny-looking fellow who takes care of the accounts—who says this really sweet thing about seeing a girl on the ferry and not approaching her and regretting it ever since then. It'll be like that, and I'll just be sore at myself for not doing it. I'm already running the little home movies in my head, you know, about what it'd be like to grab her hand and race out of here, steal a car, maybe, or just get married, have a kid, and grow old. Those sorts of things. I mean, I think most men carry around a secret library full of films they've shot of every woman they ever met. Crude little sequences strung together that help us imagine what life might be like with a particular person—buying a car, going to Disneyland, standing around in Sears while she checks the price on bath towels. Despite popular belief, guys don't mentally undress every woman they meet; they simply thread them up and run them through the imaginary film projector in their heads to see what comes of it. And that's what's happening right now. I'm watching her, my hostess, as I pour our pretend life out onto the white wall of the living room. I want to know her. Love her. Just talk to her, even, pull her out onto the pool patio and find out where she grew up, went to school, why she married that jerk who never laughs and green-lights lousy movies.

There she goes, down a hallway that probably leads to the kitchen. This is a perfect moment. Do it now or forever hate yourself. Right? But I can't. I don't know her, after all. It's their home, for God's sake; it'd probably just be loud and embarrassing and she wouldn't understand.

She couldn't. How could she realize that I've been standing here for three hours, wanting her, not even knowing what it is about her that enchants me so. She's barely spoken once. I don't love her hair, at least not the way she's wearing it, and she's shorter than the kind of women I usually go for. She's forty-five at least. At *least*. And I can't stop thinking about her. She's like a charming town you've been to yet it doesn't appear on the map, or a first-edition book that you can't really afford, but you love the dust jacket. She's that kind of person.

I guess women in general are like that, special like that. They get in your head at the strangest times and for the oddest reasons, and there they stay. Haunting you. Who can say what attracts us, makes a person like her interesting to a guy like me? I don't know, I really don't. I have no idea. But you know what? I think I'll just wander out into the kitchen for a minute, see if they have any more ginger ale. If she's there, I'll say hello. No harm in that, right? It's just hello. Anyway, I can't help myself, even if hello has paved the road to hell more often than good intentions. After all, she's a woman. A real woman. And I'm a man. It's a party. Anything can happen.

Ravishing

❖

I remember this one time, maybe three years ago, not sure, could be longer, but around there. One of the first girls we did. I mean, did like that. A black gal, half black, really, must've had a regular white mother, grandparent in there somewhere. But anyway, just this woman we found, half knocked out on coke up the street . . . asking twenty bucks a blow job. We get her into the car, both of us were there, I'm driving, gonna take her over to a storage space we rented, out in the Valley . . . ten feet by twenty, like a hundred bucks a month. Tiny place for shooting, but quiet. Nice and quiet.

So I'm at the wheel, he's in back, getting her talking . . . we're taking a risk, not really knowing anything about her, so we're tooling along, seeing if she won't open up, tell us where she lives, a boyfriend. Says she's got a kid. Family's all gone, no relations around to worry their heads off, but there's this kid.

Little girl, that's trouble, some babysitter? No, get this . . . child is eighteen months, but she leaves the little thing alone every night she's out humping and pissing around, looking for a score. Some motel, other side of town, pay by the week. Says we can go there if we want to, both of us for eighty. "She'll be asleep." We look at each other, smiling. She's the one. No question.

Our guy, guy that we favor, he's already at the place, camera set up, tripod, lights. Bitch'll think she's getting a screen test, be living in the hills soon as we get a video release. Want everything to feel just right. OK, we hear about the kid, that seems fine, few days from now she'll get passed on to welfare, adoption agency, who knows what. But we've got a live one here. So I get on the freeway, heading over, she doesn't see nothing. Head down in his lap, sucking him off. Might as well get your money's worth, right? And you know, he said later, offhanded remark one time . . . she wasn't half bad.

There's an old piece of foam or something laid out, sheet thrown over it, middle of the place. This black bitch, she's still spinning, nose all runny like it is, but she sees the three of us there, me pulling down this iron door behind us . . . her eyes flicker for a second. Comes back to join us on earth momentarily, figures "No good can come from this," she starts going off about her daughter and all, needs to get back. I jump in, calm her down, tell her she's gonna make the eighty, we just want her to do our friend, we'd like to film it, "That's how we get off." Even have her sign a release, says we won't show it in public. I thought that was a hell of a touch, settled her right down.

So we put on a piece of music, a Miles Davis kind of jazz thing, and we're talking, telling her to "go for it," all happy and saying she looks great . . . and off come the clothes. God . . . what a compliment won't get you these days, right? Snatch is out of her dress before I can get the camera focused, all swaying and pouty lips at the lens. And gradually, we add our friend, he slips in. Just sits on the mattress at first, watching her, coaxing her along . . . what a pro. Goddamn it was something! She's dancing, like I said, and all of the sudden, he whispers something, and she's bending over, ass flaring up in the picture, a finger darting in her hole. Amazing. I guess it really is true . . . everybody wants to be a star.

Pretty soon, she and the guy we use are chatting away, she's sitting on him now, pants off, and he's up in her. She's making eyes over at us, pulling faces like she was Bette Midler, not a real emotion left in her body, but these big "oohs" and "aahs" and all the rest. He's getting into it now, turns her over, pushing her down on the mattress as he's sticking her, her arms out in front holding them both up. I pull off the tripod to get down there with them, to capture it all. I mean, nothing like we planned, he's just doing her now, eyes closed, and she's kind of whimpering all of the sudden, the two of them like on their wedding night. You believe that?

I nudge him a little, and he looks up, smiling, sweat all over his forehead. And then, Jesus, like a puma or something, he pulls out of her, just straight back, and she's in the middle of a scream, it's that close. She turns a bit, "What's going on?" all over her face, and he, this guy, gets both hands around her throat. Not hard, not fighting her so much, because she's weak now, stoned like she is and fresh from, you know. She stares up at me, her eyes, and the lips curling in, the corners . . . maybe gulping down some air . . . and he just chokes the living shit out of her.

Goes on maybe thirty seconds. Close-up. Then we prop her up and each take a turn, shooting a load on her. One at a time, from a distance. Plop-plop-plop. Standing there, looking at each other afterward, we start to smile at a job well done—light from the camera humming away; it doesn't know the difference between this and a Little League game.

Dumped her out of the car, a street corner, skirt pulled back on. Could almost hear the patrol car, guys on the force twenty years, still trying to make sense of this shit. "Pimp must've gone bonkers on her . . ." I'm sure that's how it went. Just like on TV. Got back to my place and we popped in the tape. Few wine coolers, ordered a large pie, pepperoni, I think. And there she was, dancing away, the finger up herself, the two of them going at it, like it was happening all over again. We must've watched that thing, that first one we did, until two, three in the morning. And you know, that's the real beauty of all this new technology. I ever wanna see that poor cunt alive again . . . I just need to press REWIND.

Open All Night

◆

Just don't panic, he tells himself. Do not panic. This thought flashes like enemy tracer fire through his brain as he taps his forehead against the padded steering wheel of his next-year's-model car. The make isn't important. What is important, however, is that said car won't start— let's be a bit more specific about that: It's sitting in the parking lot of a strip club called The Blue Empress, and it won't start. That's right, not even turn over. Oh fuck.

He can just make out the Montblanc key ring that his wife gave him for Christmas as it catches some light filtering in from a sodium lamp overhead. The little white star twinkles up at him. How could this happen? He hadn't been inside for more than two or three hours—four at most—and now his new battery inside his new car is completely dead. Yes, maybe he'd left the lights on, OK, anybody can do that. But here, in a place like this? Unforgivable. He glances at his watch now, checking to see how much time he has left. It's ten minutes past eleven—that's P.M., folks—and he begins to understand the magnitude of his dilemma. If God doesn't get up off his benevolent ass this instant and send him some help here, he's going to end up in a hell of a spot. A bit of a pickle, as they used to say back when it was impolite to swear. If he's not home by twelve, then the entire network of lies that he has so carefully constructed around this visit will crumble like the house of cards that it is. In other words, she's not going to buy it. His wife. Third wife, by the way, so even more suspicious and prone to disbelief than his first two were.

The sound of hinges creaking open brings him back from the precipice—he swings his door open and hops out onto the pavement, trotting over two aisles to where a pair of young men are moving slowly toward a Jeep Liberty. Staggering a bit.

"'Scuse me," the man says, in a halting sort of voice. "Hello?"

One of the guys turns to him, hopping to one side as he does and putting his fists up in a defensive gesture. "Damn, dude, you spooked the shit outta me!" Both of the guys laugh at this and the man jumps in as well, trying to play along and break the ice.

"Sorry! Craziest thing . . . my car won't start. Battery, I guess."

"Yeah?" says the other one, who is shorter than the first man and maybe a year or two younger. Sporting the faintest of mustaches on his lip. In fact, it may even be the stain from a chocolate milk he had at dinner; it's that questionable. "Which one's yours?"

"Over there, the Saab convertible," he points, using his hand to lead their eyes across the lot. "Can you believe it? Got it out of the showroom—not ten miles on the thing—two weeks ago, and now this."

"Shit, yeah, I believe it," the taller one says, laughing again for no apparent reason. "You buy foreign, you pay the price."

"Yep. *Sticker* price!" says the milk-mustachioed one and they both crack up again. Even in his delicate state the man can recognize an attempt at a joke when he hears one, so he plays along and bows his head, nodding and laughing as well. Slaps at his knee, even.

"I know, I know! Guilty as charged," he says, holding his hands up in a gesture of mock surrender.

"Damn Swedes!" one of them barks. Laughter again.

"Yep. Last time I do that, I swear. They gave me a hell of a deal, though. Fully loaded, even threw a stereo in for free and I couldn't resist."

"Bullshit it was free . . . lookit you now!"

"Exactly! I should've known better, right? Nothing, and I mean nothing, comes free in this world," the man offers, hoping this will be the fraternal nugget that gets these guys to offer some assistance.

"You got that right!" says one of them, but the man misses which one it is because he is glancing over at the door to the establishment as it swings open again. An older couple—man and woman, could be husband and wife or not—slip outside and off toward a Ford. Wearing matching jackets with a kind of fringe on the sleeves. He decides to let them go and turns back to the two men in front of him.

"So, you think you can help me out?" he says. "Could probably give you each a little something for your time."

"Don't need your money," says the bigger guy, who yawns as he says it. Matter-of-factly. "It's your battery, right?"

"Yeah. I think . . ."

"Then you're flat outta luck. I don't got my cables, never carry 'em in the summer."

"Damn."

"Yep. That's fucked up, leaving your lights on."

"I know. I wasn't thinking, that's all."

"You musta got here early, huh?" the shorter one giggles, jabbing his buddy hard in the ribs. The other one gets it—after all, it was meant to be funny—and they're off to the races again, howling at the moon. A high five is even offered up at some point.

"Yeah, or in a big hurry!" chortles the other one. "Real big!"

"No, I guess I just didn't notice that they were . . ."

"Still, you pay that kinda money for a car—what'd she run you, maybe forty thou?—you'd think the damn thing could bark at you or something as you're walking away. One of those bells they got for everything else you do wrong or forget to do."

"You're right," says the man, getting a bit nervous now. Checking his watch again.

"Yep, too bad," grins the second guy, who then turns and walks off toward the other side of the SUV. The bigger of the two shrugs as he digs in his front pocket for his keys.

"Well, good luck to ya. And next time buy American, for God's sake!"

"Thanks. Yeah . . ."

The man thinks about saying something else to at least end the conversation on a high note but decides to cut his losses. He turns around and jogs back across open ground toward the Escort that is starting to pull out. He begins desperately waving his arms and manages to catch the eye of the woman with the fringe, but she frowns from her side window and turns away. A second later the Ford is nothing but taillights and exhaust. The man stops, breathing heavily, and puts his hands on his hips. An almost womanly gesture that looks strangely out of place with a flashing sign that advertises "Nude! Nude! Nude!" just behind his right shoulder. He takes another peek at his watch—a very respectable Bulova—and tries to decide on his next move. If he goes back into the club, he might be able to get someone to help him. Sure, that's possible, at least an employee or a person like that. With a few hours still to go before last call, it's iffy that he can talk a guest into coming outside with him, unless he hits it just right and the girls are on a break. No, the thing to do is try a staff member, he reasons. That's his best bet.

The man starts back over to the entrance of the place when an older gentleman in an overcoat and driving cap wanders out, looking up at the night sky. He looks like an extra from one of those English movies that Walt Disney made back in the sixties. Live-action musicals. "Good evening!" the man says, starting with a friendly wave as he approaches him. A pearly-white and costly smile tossed in to back it up.

"It certainly is that, I must say! Look at those stars," says the white-haired fellow—who must easily be in his eighties but has the poise and snap of a man fifteen years younger. "Quite glorious, a night like this one."

"Yes, absolutely," says the man, trying to keep up the sense of goodwill. "So clear when you get out here, away from the lights of the city."

"Oh, yes. Plus it's been nice these last few days, after the rain."

"Right, true. That always helps."

"Well, enjoy your evening. And there are some fine little missies in there, let me tell you, young man . . ."

The man shudders inwardly at this and tries to loop the conversation around to his needs at hand. "Oh, no, actually, I'm not going in. No, see, my car won't start, that's all. I'm stuck and I was wondering if you might . . ."

"You were inside earlier, though, correct?" The older man studies him, waiting for his answer.

The man pauses for a second, so used to lying about most things that he has to stop and think before responding. "Umm, yeah, I mean . . . for a minute. I was seeing a friend and we stopped in for a drink, but . . ."

"Then you know what I'm talking about. One of those young women had the ass of a schoolgirl—an actual girl who attends public school—and I'm not exaggerating. I'm too old for that!"

"Right. Yes, I think I did see one girl up there who was, you know . . . obviously young."

"Indeed she was. Yes, indeed-y."

"Yeah. Anyhow, do you think I could ask you something? Just a quick thing. My car is right over there and it's dead as a . . . battery's totally drained. Do you think you could . . . ?"

The older man holds up one gloved hand and wags his finger, stopping him before he can get to the other side of his question. Shuts him down completely.

"I'm waiting for a cab."

"Oh."

"Yes, at eleven-thirty sharp. I always say that to them, when I order one. 'Sharp.'"

"Huh, that's . . ."

"It's a regular service that I use, on the weekends. Quite efficient, really, and fairly clean as well, which is a plus."

"Okay, well, thanks anyway," says the man as he tries to disengage now. Headlights are approaching.

"And here it is, as promised!" notes the older man, checking his watch just to be sure. "Perfect."

"I don't mind sharing, if that helps out in some way."

"Umm, that's nice, thanks, but I need to . . ."

"Cuts the cost in half, you know. That's quite reasonable."

"No, yes, I get that part. I understand, I do, but I need my car. For, you know, work in the morning and all."

"Fine, then. I'll say good night." The octogenarian executes a strange little half bow and climbs inside the red and white Crown Victoria. The man is almost into the entrance alcove when he realizes the opportunity that is slipping away. He turns and dashes back toward the taxi, signaling for the driver to roll down his window, but the driver—obviously a legal resident in a country outside these United States—shakes a finger at him and then gestures, inexplicably, up toward the heavens. Floors it and disappears into the darkness. The man stands still as a fine cloud of dust drifts toward him, unable to decipher what has just transpired here. It would take a slew of UN interpreters and then some to make heads or tails out of that exchange.

The key slips into the ignition like a finger dipping into chocolate. Smooth and effortless. The man cranks it to the right and closes his eyes. Praying, or something very similar to that kind of religious gesture. Nothing. Shit. He figured that it was worth trying again, just in case he'd flooded the thing or whatever—this was one of the ideas his father had given him years ago, back when he used to listen to other people's advice. If you flood a car, wait a few minutes and try it again. But of course he hadn't flooded it—this probably wasn't even possible any longer, what with all the newfangled contraptions these car companies (especially European ones) were putting under the hood these days—he was just getting desperate and so he'd given it another go. For a moment—just that first second when his tendency is always to blame someone or something else—he feels like doing damage

to the car. Hurting it in some way. Jabbing his Montblanc
pen (from a different wife on a different Christmas)
through the soft black convertible top and pulling on it
with all his might. Like a soldier might have done in the
olden days, ripping his saber through the flimsy tents of
some Gypsies as his buddies were off shooting people and
burning their camp to the ground. Something like that.
His mind continues to wander across thoughts like these
for a moment—he envisions taking part in some sort of
massacre in the forests of Russia or in that cultural revolution over there in China—before a knocking sound
makes him lurch to one side. Holding his hands up near
his face, he turns and looks toward the passenger window
and into the eyes of a young woman. No more than thirty,
smiling in at him. Without thinking, he reaches out to buzz
down the window but gets nothing in return. Powerless.
He curses to himself and scrambles outside, catching his
knee on the edge of the door as he goes. Ouch.

"Hi," says the girl as she offers up another smile.
More like a grin, but it's hard to see out here in the dark.
The man grins in return and tries to speak while his mind
races back to an hour before as he was watching this same
gal hold herself upside down on a pole for a protracted
length of time. Her breasts somehow defying gravity and

pointing straight out toward him in the crowd. Honest to God, directly at him.

"Oh, hi, hello," the man finally manages to say. Stuttering a bit over the hello of it all. "You're from . . . I mean, I think I saw you. Earlier. Like, inside."

"Yeah, just finished up. My shift."

"You don't stay until closing?"

"Nah, I got a kid, so I try and get home at midnight. My mom watches her until then."

"Huh. That's . . .wow." Not a very impressive comeback, true, but it's late, the man's got car troubles, and the clock is ticking. Plus, a beautiful girl is staring at him, which has always been a point of great befuddlement to him. Well, welcome to the club. How many men have shown great aptitude at running multinational corporations or leading armies across vast deserts, only to drop to their knees like blundering Cub Scouts at the first sign of tit?

"Car trouble?" she offers sweetly. Searching for her keys.

"Yep. Brand-new and already . . . actually, I think it's my own fault," he confesses, holding up his open palms. "Left the parking lights on or something."

"Well, that's refreshing."

"What, to see a man screw up?"

"No, to hear one take the blame!" she laughs. A smile that would melt the heart of a marauding warlord. The man has no choice but to laugh along with her. He is smitten.

"I'm just that kind of guy, I suppose," he chuckles. "That's me all over!"

"Hmm, poor thing. Now what can we do about this?"

"I've been trying to . . ."

"I'd run back inside for you but I'm sure nobody's got cables in there. My car's always konking out on me. It's a junker," she offers matter-of-factly while pointing at a dented Chevy Citation at the far side of the lot. A rusty orange with an out-of-place white door on the driver's side. "I can give you a ride if you need one."

"That's very . . . " He doesn't finish this thought because it is such a lovely possibility that he refuses to let it die just yet. A quick look at his watch helps him back to his senses. "I really need to get my car back to my . . ."

"You don't wanna leave it here, is that it?"

"Pretty much, yeah."

"Don't worry, I understand." She nods, pointing with her purse toward his wedding ring. He'd forgotten to take it off when he went inside, which is usually a ritual with him. He quickly slips his left hand into his jacket pocket, trying to be casual about it but falling way short.

"Right," he mutters.

"So, listen, why don't we . . ." She looks around and studies the landscape for a moment, like some gorgeous Indian scout. That Pocahontas woman or the one who ended up on the coin. He secretly wishes he had paid a bit more attention in school now so he could make a joke about this but he lets it go. Follows her eyes as she studies the horizon.

"You know what? Why don't we just push it over there to that gas station, 'cause they're open all night. If we do that, then you can have them charge your battery and everything and I'll give you a lift."

"That's . . ." He considers the magnitude of her suggestion, this elaborate and detailed plan that seems to come with no sermon or moralizing judgment attached, and it almost brings him to tears. It really does. "It's a great idea, I mean, if you don't mind."

"Not at all. Where do you live?"

"Out in one of those subdivisions off Route Sixty-three. Stonebridge." He can see her eyes narrow for a second, calculating the distance. "I can give you gas money, if that's all right."

"That'd be really nice, " she says and her face bright-
ens right back up, like holiday lights that flicker for a
moment but have no intention of letting a family down.
"Only because tips were kinda shitty tonight and I gotta
go register tomorrow morning."

"Register?"

"For classes. I'm over at community college next semester. Just got my GED, so I figure, hey, why not?"

"Absolutely. That's really . . . so, yes, I'd happily pay
for a tank of gas. Please."

"Great! Let's do it, then."

They stand together for a moment, each in position
with the Saab poised at the top of the exit. It's a bit of
an incline so they can get up a little speed if they run.
They turn their heads from side to side in unison checking for traffic, since they'll only get one shot at it. The
Stop-N-Go is just across the street, but it's four lanes
of traffic and this road—no longer the expressway it was
before the interstate came through—still gets a lot of
truck traffic. The girl stands at the driver's door, able
to push for a second before jumping inside. The man is
ready at the rear of the vehicle, hunched over with his
sleeves rolled up. His mind is racing as he notices she
possesses those two dimples that some women have just

above their ass, like soft thumb impressions in children's clay. There's the edge of a tattoo there as well, just the hint of a cross or the like, but he can't fully make it out. He hadn't noticed it when he was watching her dance. Shaking his head, he snaps back to the job at hand and waits for her signal.

"Now!" she screams and they're off, the man pushing and grunting for all he's worth as the girl clacks along in her high heels and then hops in. Swinging the door shut behind her and steering straight as an arrow shot by Cupid himself. The man congratulates himself as he slams against the trunk again—he was smart enough to put down the top so she could easily get inside—and heaves with muscles that haven't been used in this fashion since high school. The lights of a big rig in the distance give him a sharp thrill but they make it to the gas station–food mart with no problems. Together, they've traversed the fifty yards or so of open ground with surprising speed and grace.

"Jesus, that was . . . " The man stops, unable to finish because he is winded. He leans up against his bumper for support.

"Fun, right? Good job!" says the girl, giving the man a little hug. Not anything sexual, but like a young gymnast reaching out to her coach after a fine performance on the balance beam. "Now you're all set. Got yourself covered . . ."

"Yeah," the man puffs, still sucking down air in an attempt to regain some composure. "You do this often?" he jokes, trying to keep it light.

"Once or twice," she murmurs. "A couple times."

"Oh."

"I mean, if somebody needs help you give it, right?"

"I suppose . . ."

"You'd do the same thing," she whispers, not checking to see if he agrees. Without thinking, the man reaches out for her and returns her hug. She allows it, but this time he can feel that she is pulling back a touch. Just a bit, but the way she might if she had just been pressing her backside against his lap and he'd tried to slip a bill inside her g-string. "If she makes contact then it's OK" is the hard and fast rule at the club—apparently it applies outside The Blue Empress as well.

He waves to her from the blind corner that leads to his cul-de-sac. The girl has wisely dropped him off a block or so from his house and is now executing a U-turn that will point her back in the direction of the highway and, eventually, into town. Their eyes meet for a second and she blows him a kiss. He moves to mirror the gesture but she reaches over to fiddle with her stereo—playing a kind of black person's music at a deafening volume that he could barely understand—and misses his sendoff. In another minute she turns left onto Mill Hollow Drive and vanishes into the murk. The man can see that a light is on upstairs in the colonial he calls home, but he lingers for a moment on the sidewalk, knowing that he will get one last view of the Citation when it reaches the gates at the front of the property. It will only be a fleeting glimpse, but he decides to wait. He turns up the collar of his jacket—a lightweight Brooks Brothers sports coat that was a gift—and rises up on his tiptoes. Watching.

Full Service

◆

I can't tell what color her nails are, not completely, because of the dirt and oil smeared across her fingers. They're soaked in the stuff, actually, but it's only because she's changing my fluids at the moment. Brake, transmission, wiper. And the coolant, too; she's also taking care of that. She seems very efficient, this little technician of mine. Not that she's one of those specialized people, some Mr. Goodwrench or something—though actually she would have to be a Mrs. Goodwrench or at least a Ms. Goodwrench, things being what they are in the world—no, she works locally at this mom-and-pop garage that I frequent, down the road from my lake cottage. "Frequent" in that it's convenient for me, not that I'm this longtime customer or anything. Well, I suppose my family is, since my father used to come here when he first bought the cottage. And believe me, back then there wouldn't have been any girl changing your oil or anywhere near your car, for that matter, oh no. And the original guy, the owner, he'd had daughters, too, but they didn't work in the shop area. The oldest one, this buxom redhead, she maybe ran the cash register during her last few summers of high school, but that was about it. And even that was a *maybe*.

But now, a generation or so later, they go and rename the joint Happy Lube and have one of those big dancing air-filled gorillas on the roof—what does that have to do with oil, I ask you?—and young women parading around in tight uniforms and working on your car. Well, OK, no, it's not exactly like that, I'm exaggerating for effect, but it's close. The name and jungle animal are true, but she, this girl I'm staring at right now, may be the only female employee on the premises. But they do seem very open to the idea, very laissez-faire in their approach to preventative car maintenance. But, as I say, they're convenient, so I keep my big mouth shut. Not that she's doing a bad job, either, from what I can tell. Seems to know her stuff, if a little "by the book." No, she's doing fine, I shouldn't complain. One greasy handprint that I can see—on the right front quarter panel—but it's no big deal. And anyway, I'm sure she'll wipe that off before she's through. No doubt.

We keep catching each other's eye as she works, me as I'm pretending to read something in a *Field & Stream* magazine and her as she pulls the air filter out for a closer inspection. I could be leafing through a nice copy of *Newsweek* or something, but I grabbed the manliest periodical out of the bunch, trying to make up for some imagined deficit within myself, since I am surrounded by young, rugged boys covered in grime as they work on engines and talk about sports. And this girl, of course. I'm doing this outdoorsy show partly for her. I even laugh out loud once or twice at an editorial piece about bass fishing, just to add a bit of aural effect to the proceedings. She glances over and smiles at me when I do, so I push it and snicker once more, a bit further on when I hit a passage that highlights the author's travails at selecting the proper lure. Ho, ho, hilarious. But she responds again, wiping her cheek with the back of one hand and leaving the most adorable little smear of grease just under her left eye.

It's the kind of thing you'd love to just go over and wipe off with the edge of your shirt, clean it off and look into her eyes as you're doing it. Which leads to this long, movie-style kiss, all fireworks and rotating cameras and whatever it is they do out there in Hollywood to make you feel funny inside when two actors embrace. Of course, most men would then carry it a step further and have her say some stupid dialogue for a minute and then remove her clothes. Drop to her knees and all kinds of other stuff, too, or maybe even get a few other women involved in the festivities. That's the way a lot of guys' minds work, but not mine. Nope. I only get as far as the oil spot and the kiss, and then I snap out of it. Right back to reality. This is partly due, of course, to the fact that she's suddenly standing right over me. This girl mechanic. Standing in front of me and smiling down, a clipboard held loosely in one hand.

"You're all set," she offers in a surprising voice. Not that it's surprising that she can speak, no, it's just that she sounds lively and educated and full of something. Life, I guess. She seems bubbling over with life and makes me happy to be living it in the process. Not a bad day's work for my little grease monkey.

I follow her up to the register to pay and get my computerized breakdown of services. As I'm putting away my Amex (member since '87) and she's slipping my receipt into a flimsy red envelope, she adds: "If there's any problem, give us a call and we'll hook you up." Now, I suppose that is young person's lingo for "We can fix it," but most of it flows right past me like today's rock and roll music. I get the gist of what she's saying, though, and something about her manner, some twitch across her brow, seems to suggest a world of possibilities waiting just outside these cinderblock walls. Something girlish and playful and calling to me, if only I'd care to respond.

"Okeydokey," I toss back. "And who should I ask for?" A thumb points firmly and proudly to a grimy patch that has been hand-sewn onto her striped shirt. "Tammy," it reads. *Tammy* with a traditional *y* ending. Nice.

"So, I should just request you, then?"

"Sure, go for it."

"Really?"

"Yep, gimme a call. Anytime." She holds this next look just long enough for me to heed her advice, and I still don't know why. But I do, I go for it.

"Well, I will then."

"Cool."

"Alrighty."

"Great."

"Or maybe you'd like to call me . . ."

"Huh?"

"I'm just saying, I mean, if you want to." She says nothing after that, but her nothingness just spurs me on, because if we men possess genius for any one thing, it is the innate and uncanny ability to misread, misinform, and misunderstand. It's our collective gift and curse. She smiled at me, after all; that must mean something. A smile is never simply a smile. I grab the red folder from her hands—carefully brushing two of my fingers across hers as I do it—and tear off a corner. Snatching a pen from among the twenty or so resting in a Styrofoam cup on the counter, I scribble my cell number down with a bravado that I usually reserve for picking up the tab when my supervisor is with me at lunch. With a little swagger I push the paper into the girl's palm, and as a capper, I even lean forward and clean that errant smudge from her delicate cheekbone. Tammy's cheekbone. I hold the offending smear up to her astonished eyes as a kind of exclamation point, to seal the deal. Afterward, I grab my keys from her outstretched fingers and shoot a look back over my shoulder. Whispering loudly to "Call me."

As I'm fighting to pull that stupid paper floormat out from under my sandals, I become aware of a growing rumble nearby. Not a cacophony of voices, exactly, but a kind of rising chorus that makes me look up. I spot Tammy with some of the other employees across the way, pointing at my car and talking. Well, laughing might be more truthful, but it is the delicate mixture of pointing and laughter that turns into a general blur of humiliation by the time it reaches my retina. I take this in and digest it, swallow it all down along with my pride, and twist the key savagely in the ignition. Before the engine can really even catch I stomp on the gas, bolting forward through the opening in my late-model Cutlass. I catch Tammy's eye one last time as I drive off, and I notice that she is crying, big harsh tears of merriment that rain down onto the unfinished concrete at her feet. And that's what gets me, those tears of hers. That's what really gets my goat about this whole incident.

I slam the shifter thing into P and jump out, just to show my little audience back there who's boss. I begin to walk around the vehicle, inspecting it. After a moment, I stop near the front right tire and examine it a bit more closely. A fine greasy handprint, highly visible, is still there. Well, well. A chink in Tammy's youthful armor has just presented itself. Calmly now, with absolute resolve and composure, I dial the number on the receipt that I'm still clutching in one whitened fist. I am careful to add the area code, as one must frustratingly do these days. And then I wait. I wait until a male voice answers: "Hello, Happy Lube, may I be of service?"

"Yes, you may. I just received your Blue Ribbon Lube and I'm not satisfied with the work. Could you send Tammy out, please? I'm right out front."

I can see a commotion beginning inside, with several faces peering out through the polarized glass at me. I'm sure that I even hear her voice at one point—Tammy's— as she says, "No way!" or something else equally negative and childish. Finally, a young man, no more than nineteen and sporting those sideburns that boys are wearing these days (and, if I'm not mistaken, he may even attend the technical institute where I teach), emerges from the exit and wanders toward me. Cleaning his hands carefully on a Happy Lube rag as he approaches.

"Can I help you?"

"I asked for Tammy."

"Umm, she's on a break."

" I see. A break, huh? At nine A.M."

"Uh-huh."

"Fine, just as well, because she's lousy at her job."

"What's the problem?"

I smirk, pointing at the offending mark near the headlight.

"She left that."

"What, the handprint there?"

"Yes, I just waxed the thing and I'd like you people to take care of it."

"Fine, whatever." The boy moves over and chammies the oil spot away in a flash. He does a passable job, but nothing more. "Is that all?" he says, looking down.

"Yes."

"Okay, then."

"Good. Right."

I turn to get back into my Oldsmobile when I hear, rather softly, "You sure you don't wanna gimme your number?"

I turn and face him, both surprised and outraged by his snot-nosed boldness. "What did you say?"

Instead of running, though, or displaying the usual fear that follows a show of bravery, the kid turns to me and smiles. Just smiles right at me. Long and slow and without a flicker of emotion. Oh, I get it now, of course. He *likes* her. For God's sake, this is turning into a farce, some European farce that undoubtedly ends with me locked out of my hotel room with my trousers down around my ankles. Not literally, of course, but you get the picture. A minute passes, then another. We perform the requisite standoff, then move away from each other simultaneously—he back to the shop and me to inspect his handiwork. I kneel down and look at my fender, really studying it now. It seems OK, but I'll need to polish the whole car later; I mean, that's obvious. She may've even put a slight ding in the paint—no doubt with her class ring or something—but I won't know for sure until I buff the thing out.

As I'm deciding this, I slowly notice that a young girl on a Schwinn has stopped near me. She is sweaty and chewing on a strand of red licorice—one of those "Super Rope" things—with the wrapper still twisting and clinging to it. She is silent. Watching me. My eyes narrow, then I jump to my feet and make a little move toward her, raising my voice as I do.

"What the HELL are you looking at?! Get out of here!"

Her face twitches, eyes widening as her tiny brain tries to process the attack. It almost looks as if she's going to say something in response, but she bursts into tears instead and hurriedly pedals off. I watch her go, satisfied with at least one normal human response today, then turn back to my Olds again and crouch down. Stroking its gleaming paint. Cooing softly into the wheel well and promising to wash this entire episode away when we get back to our little home.

Loose Change

◈

It isn't a circle. Not exactly that. More like a broken ring then, with another lighter X-ray of itself to one side. Both symbols seem to have been burned into the leather, but white-hot, so heated that they have left pale impressions of themselves rather than the charred, blackened versions one might expect. It is almost a brand of sorts, like those found on the hides of cattle in the Wild West of the nineteenth century, but upon inspection can be seen to come from within. The marks are on the inside.

She pulls the wallet closer now, to inspect it a bit more carefully. It's one of the two she's given him over the years, a birthday or Father's Day gift that had, at the time, been much appreciated. Items had been transferred almost immediately from the previous billfold into the new one, as if to physically display approval. Driving license, cash money, that lucky Mexican peso that he had found in the dirt of a roadside rest stop on the way to San Diego. Looking at it now, the wallet in question, she can't decide if this is the first one or the second—black leather isn't very forthcoming with details. But she had given it to him, of this she is certain.

How long would it take to create a mark like this one? A year, maybe three? Longer? And in strange, sporadic intervals. True, he travels once or twice a month in his work, but only for days at a time. No more than a week. It would take quite a while for wear of this kind to make itself known. Many repetitions. If she lets herself drift for a moment, she can imagine the often-repeated scenario, see him pulling the ring off his finger in the airport lounge and then tucking it safely away. Or perhaps earlier. In the taxi or even just as he slips out the front door. For once the deception begins, one never knows how quickly the disease may spread.

She sits down on the edge of their California queen, slumping almost, to rest on the plaid comforter that adorns this bed in their master suite. A first-floor master, the kind she'd always dreamed of when they were younger and poorer and happier. Much, much happier than this. This moment in which she has now discovered the circle. A circle that will surely lead to the fiery depths of hell as quickly as any path in the pages of Dante. She looks at it again, this insignificant coin pocket that now seems to hold the key, the missing key to all the silences and layovers and business trips and the slow, seeping death that has crept into her marriage. Into the very fiber of her life. And bones. She studies it, the ringlet, turning it this way and that as she holds it up to the skylight overhead. Not very scientific, to be sure, but she's not operating in the world of science right now. No. Her thoughts are being fueled by pain and anger and sorrow and doubt. A kind of science, perhaps, the science of emotions, but not a very practical one. Not one that wins any Nobel prizes or cures any cancer or helps any young children sit up straight and walk again. This empirical path leads in one direction only—to the land of regret.

She then makes an effort to squash these thoughts, these random assaults on her own self and relationship. Maybe it is the mark of a coin. Unlikely, she reasons, but certainly a theory worth exploring. Worth seeing it through before jumping in the Benz and driving downtown and confronting him in his office, anyway. Before bursting in on a business lunch or a round of golf, tripping over her own inappropriate shoes as she swings this rogue calfskin pouch wildly about the air in front of him. Yes, it's well worth a try. She then trots off to the kitchen, making her way to the enamel jar where all loose change is dumped upon arrival home. Both he and she have turned this little action into a kind of practiced ritual. And rituals are nice; they're lovely, they signal a connection between two like beings. Crawling back up that circular drive and parking and walking through those doors again and dropping a handful of loose change into the jar somehow says, "Honey, I love you," through these hollow, empty halls. To be sure, it is a language known only to desperate, middle-aged ears, but a language nonetheless.

A quarter won't do it. A penny has already been tried. The dime, by quick process of elimination and by virtue of its size, seems improbable. Only the nickel can save her now. Save both of them, actually. From what she is not wholly sure, but the notion of being saved is a comforting one. She turns the coin over and over between her fingers, trying to focus and study it. Looking at that profile of Jefferson. The cute little ribbon at the back of his head, the base of his neck. How many people did this fine president save in his day, anyway? Thousands, no doubt, in some fashion or another—so why not now, in her time of great need? Why not, indeed?

The five-cent piece is held to the outside of the wallet first, to give some rough estimation of its size. Shape. Dimension. There, look at that. It is not a horrible fit, if not a perfect one. She is unconvinced by this little test, however, this rough application of matter and mass. Perhaps it's better to check it from the inside, from deep within, where the offending roundness first began. Yes, that's it. An ideal solution. She drags the entire enterprise off to the bathroom now, where better lighting exists. A makeup mirror, normally used for tweezering and brushing and flossing and plucking, will also be added to the mix. Help with the deed of unmasking the villain or clearing his good name. To find out the brutal, honest, ugly truth about her chosen mate. Whatever that may mean.

Holding the coin in place with a free finger, she leans in to get a better look. Her reading glasses have to be adjusted this way and that because of the mirror's glare, but that's to be expected. This entire undertaking is new to her and a degree of improvisation is not only required but is to be expected. Yet from the outside, it is impossible to tell. Yes. It could be that a nickel has been the culprit, and for this she is most relieved. Or, at least, very relieved. "Most" relieved would only be possible with a clean bill of moral health for her spouse, and this she cannot provide. Not yet. Not at this time.

He'll be home soon, of course. She knows this, sitting perched on the edge of the toilet seat. A wooden toilet seat, actually, one that he'd spotted in a *SkyMall* catalog during one of his many plane trips across the country. Or perhaps on his way to Europe. Short bursts of travel that come up without notice and with only the tiniest look of betrayal in his eyes. Dancing somewhere within his pupils. "I'm going but I really don't have to. They don't require it, but I want to. I'd *like* to do it. I offered to, in fact." This is what she always dreams of on the evening that he leaves. Not of palm tree beaches or missed office parties or even that he is falling into the arms of some younger siren, no. It is simply the nightmare of loss. A Cassandra-like vision of the here and now, a vision that says, "Yes, my dear, it's true. He'd rather be anywhere but here with you." He'd seen it, this toilet fixture on which she finds herself, on page 37 and had called the 1-800 number from his business class seat with the magazine open on his lap. He'd liked it that much, this throwback to a different era. Back in the day when the bathroom was not connected to the house, or at least the house proper. It had come by FedEx and been waiting for him when he returned. He came back from Cologne with a box of Godiva chocolates for her (the smaller box, like the ones they sell in Lord & Taylor now) and had gone straight down the hallway with the wooden seat cradled under one arm. Dropped his bags in the bedroom and installed it himself. And was the first to use it, as well. And now here she sits on it, staring at his wallet and wondering. Wondering just what the answer may be. The answer to the puzzle that is this circle. This infernal circle on his coin pocket that carries with it the power to change the world. Her world, at least.

In the end she decides that only his ring can answer to the charges. Only his wedding band, the one she had picked out with her mother back in Akron so many years ago, at the jewelry store on Wicker Street that her second cousin's father owned. This alone would be able to do the trick. So now she'll have to wait. Wait for him to return. Or return the call, at least, the one she'd already placed to his cell phone. Then wait longer still, for him to turn back around on the freeway, maybe down near the exit to the outlet mall or even later, where the traffic bottlenecks near

the Sacred Heart Hospital. Maybe even there. She's looked
through the pockets and cracks and crannies of the thing
earlier, to see what else might be found. It doesn't surface
very often, you see, this wallet of his. He keeps it deep
within his pocket at all times, even in his bathing suit, which
looks peculiar but she never says a word about it. That's
what had made her curious about it, after all. Its absence.
But that's the case with anything, isn't it? When you know
something is there, has been for so long, and then for some
reason it simply goes away, well, you can't help but notice.
You realize when it disappears. A bird on your lawn, a
friend from church, an ice-cream flavor down at the
Baskin-Robbins. Your husband's love. When these things
go and you still desire them, you tend to notice. And this
was the case with his wallet.

In the old days, those heady prechildren days of possibility, his billfold would spend the night on their chest
of drawers. Always in the same spot, always placed there
before bed. A ritual. But slowly, within the last six years
or so, the wallet had disappeared, burrowed down into
the man's trousers, never to see the light of day. Not
around her, anyway. And this—not at first, no, not that—
had finally led her to this very moment, this haunted
hunting through his things. The lowest place she could

imagine ever finding herself. Pawing through his drawers, digging through his sport coats looking for a clue. Some clue to this hopeless place that her heart has rented out for the summer. At the corner of despair and desperation. Just across the tracks from damnation. You know the place, or if you don't, you've heard of it. This is where the journey of her married life has led her—crouched down on a wooden toilet seat and searching through her husband's belongings.

Now, when he returns home to retrieve the offending wallet, she'll be ready for him. Ready to pounce while he's still behind the wheel, without letting him even stand so he can utilize his height against her. He always uses this against her in an argument, but not this time. "This will be a full-on attack," she surprises herself by saying aloud, and she begins to steel herself to the notion. Shove the thing right in his face and demand an answer. Better yet, grab the ring from his hand as it dangles out the window, the way it always does when he drives on balmy days like this. Grab it and run off across the lawn before he knows what hit him—if she can make it around the side yard, back to the pool house and lock herself in, then she stands a decent chance of finding the truth. A moment where she can test the ring against the spots. The circles.

These circular wells of truth that stand in sharp relief to the rest of his wallet.

It's not that the truth would even start to suggest that he's done anything wrong, at least in the biblical sense or in a court of law. Not at all. It wouldn't immediately say that he has cheated on her or that another woman or man or whatever he's drawn to—she hardly knows him, she fully realizes now, even after twenty-some years—is waiting out there, ready to join his life. It merely states, in no uncertain terms, that he is open to it. That on the road, he prefers to appear a single man. Unconnected to her. Alone. And this tears at her very soul, this idea. Her ring has grown tight and tarnished on her gnarled left hand, never even removed during shampooing or gardening. Not once, even during those painful months of pregnancy when her digits ballooned to twice their normal size, did she take off her wedding band. And what she's found, or believes she's found, paints a very different portrait of her marriage than the one she carries in the family room of her mind. The den of her dreams. This deceit in his wallet speaks of another life, a life that he has lived out for years now, happily without her.

The sound of wheels rumbling across gravel makes her jump. Stand up. Tense. It is now or never, she supposes, this hideous moment of truth. To let him enter the house would be fatal, like lowering the bridge and inviting the Vikings in for a cup of tea. She knows the advantage is hers and must be taken. So out the bathroom door she goes, padding across the Berber carpet on the landing and heading down the stairs. Plunging into a world she doesn't understand and is unprepared for. Ill-equipped and unfamiliar with notions of separation and divorce and alimony. Seen them on TV, to be sure, and heard of one-time friends at the club doing it, but it is nothing she was raised on or cares to know anything about, thank you very much. Not until this moment, anyhow. But on she scoots, along the hallway and out onto the porch. She stares down at him, sitting there in his El Dorado all balding and tanned and distant. The man she loves. And then it happens. The gesture. An impatient wave from him that unwittingly heralds her attack. She sees it—that dismissive "hurry up already" shake of the wrist—and she takes a breath. A long breath, there at the top of the steps, with tears starting to collect in the corners of her eyes. His snapping fingers call her to battle. Snap-snap-snap. And then down she rushes, and down and down. Headfirst and growling, moving with surprising urgency toward the big Cadillac. She sees that her husband responds by desperately trying to raise the tempered window as she approaches. Finger tapping the metal button repeatedly.

For a small woman, she hits the door with enormous speed and power. The car rocks on its springs and her husband is tossed hard to one side. Before he can gather himself she attacks again, throwing herself like a rabid dog against the half-opened window. Again and again. And then again. Bang-bang-bang. And for the first time in their marriage—perhaps even in his life—the man senses fear within himself. Feels a squirt of urine shoot out into his briefs. In another situation he would throw open the door and spill out onto the ground, ready for a fight. But not this time. No. For as his wife continues to press herself against the glass and shriek at him, he can only grab the webbing of his safety belt in horror. Leaning for all he's worth to his right. Holding on for dear life.

Switzerland

◆

You only become aware of her after twenty or thirty minutes in the shop. Maybe even longer. God knows how many times she's glanced over at you already, but she finally catches your eye when you drift over to a pile of old magazines. A stack of *Life* and *Look,* each one trapped in a faded sleeve of plastic and left there to rot. It's Gene Tierney's face on the cover of one that you notice first— she's an actress, an old-time movie actress, in case any of you are wondering—and she's someone that you've always liked. Not that she was ever as famous as some of those ladies or is remembered in the same way as a Liz

Taylor today, but she had something special about her. Oh yes, in her eyes. That's what you liked about her. And this girl, the one who seems to have been watching you all this time, well, she's a little bit like her in some way. That Gene Tierney person.

There's no reason why you should go over there and introduce yourself to her, so you don't. Why should you? This isn't the kind of place where you'd do a thing like that, slide over there and make small talk. No. It isn't some sports bar in Chicago or a club in South Beach— this is a two-bit sort of antique store just off the main highway that caught your eye as you were waiting at the single traffic light in the center of town. A billboard attached to the roof of a local restaurant—called The Rustler's Roost, if you must know—grandly stated that here resided the "Single Largest Antique Mall in the Tri-State Area." Well, well, you thought, now that is something. Not that you're one of those garage sale freaks who goes from house to house, neighborhood to neighborhood looking for old G.I. Joe clothes or Roseville Pottery. Absolutely not. But as you were sitting there and waiting for the green, you idly tried to figure out which three states that sign might be referring to. Which led to you wondering just what treasures might indeed be hidden

away in Herb's Antique Grotto. Because if a name like
that can't draw you in, well then, nothing ever could.

Your attention shifts back to the girl now, who, when
you really give her the once-over, can't be more than
twenty. Twenty-two, tops. Definitely out of school, high
school, anyway, but this is probably her first job. Real job,
at least, if you can call sitting on a stool and writing up sales
receipts by hand on a pad of lined paper a "job." She
doesn't even have a cash register, you note, just one of those
metal boxes that has a handle on it and a slot in the front
for a little key. More like a child's toy than a proper space
to house the cash of a working establishment, but that's
the kind of place this is. Seems to be, at least, in a town
like this one. Not that you should expect any more than
this, though, as you well know. These communities up
here—cities and towns and villages—that make up this
part of the state are pretty rustic. And that's being generous. A thought like this can easily lead you back to wondering why your parents would ever choose to retire up
here, whether they bought property near the lake back in
the sixties or not—dirt cheap, as the old man is proud to
say at every family gathering—so you drop it and go back
to browsing through the stacks of comic books and Coca-
Cola bottles. You promise yourself that this is the last sum-

mer that you're going to make this drive again—you'll buy them a pair of cheap tickets online next year and fly them down to stay with you—and leave it at that.

It's about time for you to toss another smile over at the girl when you spot it. Next to a Betty Crocker pie pan and a framed tribute to John Wayne—a triptych that has been hand-painted by a local artist—it flashes up at you like the Holy Grail itself. Caught for a moment in the light from a nearby window—a trick or refraction and timing—and you literally have to shield your eyes for a moment to look at it. Now, your first instinct is to back away, to act like you haven't even noticed it yet, in case the girl is still watching you. You steal a glance over at her and are relieved to see that she has returned to her battered copy of V. C. Andrews—one about some children in an attic somewhere who are being naughty. You circle back to the table quite casually, picking up a baseball mitt as you walk along. When you get close enough you lean down for a moment, just for a moment, to make sure that you haven't been mistaken. Seen a mirage. You pick it up slowly, turning it over in your hands, marveling at the fact that it hasn't rusted out at the hinges or lost any of its color. But no, a Six Million Dollar Man lunch box and not a dent in sight. Eager now, you snap open the lid to see if by some lucky chance the thermos might still be inside. It sparkles up at you like the Hope diamond, nestled firmly beneath the wire hooking mechanism that you remember so well. What a find. What manna from heaven. It's the vintage 1974 version, too, not the '78, which was much inferior, in your mind, to this little jewel. Your childhood floods back to you as you stand there, rushing down and over you like spring runoff high in the Rockies. School buses and recess and holidays and sidewalk lemonade stands swirl around in your head for a moment, causing you to nearly swoon. A thing like this, a simple piece of pressed metal and plastic, can transport a grown man like yourself back to your youth like something out of an H. G. Wells story. Amazing but true. You stand as living proof of the power of memory. Memory and memorabilia.

You decide to do it quickly, decisively, rather than dance around for the next half hour, pretending to buy other items and haggle over their prices, all the while trying to keep the girl from noticing the value of what you really desire. You step up to the counter and set the lunch box down. Look up into her eyes as she pulls away from her paperback and turns to you and the business at hand. She smiles at you—she's definitely cute, this idle country lass—and then looks down at your purchase. Even turns it over for a second before frowning. She pulls it a bit closer to herself and opens it. You can't help it—your left hand instinctively shoots out to protect the thing but you catch yourself and pretend that you're only stretching. She may not believe it, but at least you've done what you can to repair the damage. With a sweeping, decisive gesture she places the lunch pail under the counter and smiles at you, shaking her head.

"Sorry about that, our mistake."

"What's that mean?" you say, confused. "What mistake, where?"

"It got left out there by accident."

"I'm sorry, I'm lost. What are you . . . ?"

"Not for sale."

You don't want to panic yet, not quite yet. Remember, she's only a child, a small-town girl with a high school education and one of those flowery peasant shirts on. You've been here before. You know how to handle this. The likes of her.

"Umm, forgive me, I'm not following you. How can that not be for sale? It's out on the showroom floor."

"The what?" She looks at you like you just landed your spacecraft in the center of the grotto itself. "I don't understand."

"I'm saying that the lunch box there, that thing you just put under the counter, was out on a table and next to a bunch of other stuff." You point back over your shoulder, thinking that a simple physical illustration will help her get up to speed. "All that junk over there—I don't mean *junk* like it's lousy stuff, just that it's, you know what I mean—it's all available to purchase, right?"

"Yep. That's our markdown bin."

"OK," you say, "exactly my point. That's where I found it. Over there."

"Yeah, but it's a mistake. It wasn't supposed to be there."

"And why's that?"

"It's my brother's. I guess he left it there when he got home from school. He usually comes in here and says hi and stuff before doing his homework. Anyway, sorry."

"I see," you mutter, letting it slip out of your mouth like a death sentence. Hold on now, keep it together, you think, we're not done here yet. Some important info has just come your way, and you instantly try to assess the situation. Force an advantage. The item belongs to a boy—a child, really—and that can certainly come in handy, plus you now know that this young woman isn't even an actual employee but the daughter of the owner. Of Herb himself. If need be, you can always ask to speak to her superior (Dad) and get down to it, mano a mano. You let a little sigh of relief escape your lips and turn your attention more fully back to her. "So, it's your brother's, huh?"

"Yeah. He's always doing that, leaving his crap around," she offers, flashing a set of teeth that make her the former cheerleader that she undoubtedly is. "We tell him not to— Mom does, anyhow—but he thinks this is, like, some public park or whatever in here. Running up and down the aisles and stuff; he's so annoying."

"Hmm. I see." You've got to be careful here—not too eager but somewhat insistent. Use a bit of the old "big city" charm that comes so naturally to you. "Do you mind if I see it again? Just for a second."

Naturally she's suspicious and only holds it out to you from a distance, allowing you to do exactly what you've asked for: see it. You grin at her literal application of your request, then laugh. Not broadly or forced, but with the natural grace that your laugh has taken on during your adult years.

"I'm sorry," you say, "I meant could I actually hold it again?"

Reluctantly she obliges you but does not return to her novel. She only really hands it over when two older women in pantsuits and matching sunglasses barge into the room from an entrance across the way. They arrive with a clatter of dishes and swinging purses and the girl's attention is momentarily stolen. She studies you one more time—you'd think she was handing you the keys to the palace treasury, the way she's acting—before putting the pail into your hands and wandering off to assist the interlopers.

You study the sides of the metal rectangle reverentially, as if on bended knee deep in the bowels of the Vatican. Every episode that is depicted on it is both instantly recalled and savored. The man himself, Steve Austin—played by the actor Lee Majors—hovering as a large disembodied head over several moments of bionic splendor: racing a horse on foot; bending a piece of railroad track with his bare hands; leaping over an oncoming car. On the backside, he is uprooting a tree and hitting two thugs while his good friend, Oscar Goldman, looks on. You scan the individual pictures that grace the spine of the thing and your knees begin to quiver. You check the girl again, who is now a good fifty yards away behind a tower of board games. Surprising even yourself, you glance toward the nearest exit and calculate the distance. You could make it out of the room in ten seconds, no question, and that would be walking. At an even pace. Something inside forces you to dig into a front pocket for a twenty-dollar bill—you weren't thinking of stealing the thing, for God's sake!—as a voice from behind causes you to stumble forward. Bumping your right knee against the wood-paneled counter.

"Hey, gimme my thingy!"

You turn to face a boy of around ten, hovering right behind you. Too close for it to be proper, actually, but it's no doubt because you're holding his property. His dirty little fingers reach up toward the item, making impatient half-circles in the air.

"Hi, kid, what's your name?" you offer.

"Timmy," he snorts, still with his fists aloft.

"You own this place?"

The irony of this notion is broad enough for even the boy to appreciate and a huge grin spreads over his freckled cheeks like a chunk of watermelon hitting the pavement. "Yep!" he laughs, snorting a touch as he does. His sister shoots a look at him from around a spire of Golden Books—the kind you read as a kid, like *The Poky Little Puppy* and that sort of deal—and then gets back to helping the ladies. "This here is my store."

"That's cool. I thought some guy named Herb owned it, but now I know better."

"Herb's my daddy. He's Herb."

"Oh, I see, so, you just run it for him . . ."

"No! I'm a kid," the boy says, smiling again. "I was just kidding before."

"Got it. But you do own this lunch box here," you say, bringing this Norman Rockwell moment back into sharp relief. "This is yours, that's what your sister said."

"She's stupid, she doesn't even know nothing."

"No?"

"Uh-uh. I got five of 'em, one for each day of the week!"

"Wow. Cool. That's really nice. So, which ones?"

"Huh?"

"What other types do you have?"

"Oh, umm, let's see . . . I got a Scooby-Doo, and a Dukes of Hazzard, and this Disney one that has a bunch of different characters on it, and one from a show that was called *Gunsmoke*—that's a Western—and then that there. The Million Dollar Man kind."

You catch yourself before you scream right in his jelly-smeared face. Actually feel your teeth having to dig into your tongue and forcing your mouth closed before you can reprimand him right here on his own property. You blink a few times, forcing a grin as you say, very politely, "It's actually called 'Six Million Dollar Man.' Six. Not just a 'Million.' I mean, just so you know."

"Whatever," he says, starting to act a bit impatient now. "It's a good one, that's all I know about it. I like that guy right there, with the tree branch."

"That's him, the . . . Bionic Man," you say, fighting back tears of some kind. "He was a test pilot and he works for the government now, after a horrible accident. See, they rebuild him. He's got nuclear . . ."

"Lemme have it a second, I'll show you the drink thingy," the child offers as he puts his arms in the air again. You know this will be the end of it if you give in now, once his dirty fists get a grip on the blue handle again. It's now or never, you reason. Do it now.

"You ever see the show, like, on reruns or anything?"

"Nope. We don't have cable," he says and stares at you. "Now, gimme."

"So . . . wait, let me ask you something here," you stammer, trying to get your bearings as you again measure the space between you and the nearest doorway. It would be a broken-field run, no question, what with all the tables and cardboard standees of sports heroes in the way, but you could make it. You feel confident about this. "How about selling it? You ever thought about that?"

"Why? We got a whole shelf of 'em over there," he states, pointing toward a back wall. "All different ones, too."

"Yeah, but is there another of these, the 'Six Million Dollar Man' kind?"

"Dunno. No, probably not, but that one's mine . . ."

"What about if I gave you, like, say, twenty dollars?" You throw it out there like chum to a shark, hoping it lands with the intended impact. The boy sniffs and blinks for a second, processing this. What you didn't figure into the equation—how could you?—is that this is Herb's boy and he's no idiot. Well, he comes dangerously close to being an idiot, but an idiot savant when it comes to other people's junk and, therefore, dangerous when trying to wheel and deal with. The kid's eyes narrow and he shows his top row of teeth. One incisor missing. There's only one direction to go in now, you figure, and that's forward. Go for broke because this fellow is on to your game and his sister continues to watch you as she lifts a set of used car mats down from an overhead space. The older women cooing at the various colors and shapes.

"Why don't we make it fifty?" you say, even before you realize it.

"Ummm . . . lemme get my sister," he fires back and holds up his palm toward his property. Fully expecting it this time. You drop the twenty onto his sweaty flesh instead, changing tactics in a last-ditch effort.

"Oh, and could you get me change for this? Thanks a lot."

Timmy is thrown by this one—he's been raised to be helpful with the customers—and so he nods and wanders off, heading toward where his sister is standing on a short folding ladder. At the moment his head disappears behind a display of lamp shades you dart for the door, moving with a purpose. It's almost a jog, if you're honest with yourself, and you decide to stop for no one.

Six steps from the archway you meet a mountain range of a man—any doubt as to whether or not he is Herb is removed at seeing his name sewn on the front of his vest—who greets you with a broad smile and a kind of half salute. "Howdy, young fella, need any help?" You drop the lunch pail to your hip and turn slightly away, covering the booty as best you can while you keep moving.

"Just looking, thanks," you stammer as you clear the door frame and start reaching for the emergency exit.

"Well, come back and see us!" his throaty voice booms out behind you, turning all the other heads in the place. You try to nod but can only keep walking at this point. Picking up the pace as you begin fumbling for the rental keys in your pocket with your free hand.

The sound of churning gravel seems like something from a movie sound track as you fly out of the parking lot, barely missing the back end of an older-model Lincoln Mark IV. You're starting to breathe more easily now, sweating still but actually feeling a little like Lee Majors saving yet another day. Or, maybe not quite that heroic, if you're honest with yourself. No, maybe a bit more like Steve McQueen at the end of *The Great Escape.* Except that you are not going to fall off your motorcycle right now. No. You are going to make it home. You can feel it.

Only a flash of orange in your rearview mirror betrays this certainty—when you take a look you see the tiny figure of Timmy running behind you now, desperately moving through the tall grass that grows along the shoulder of the road in front of his family home. The sister—so alive and Gene Tierney-like in her girlish blouse a half hour ago—follows closely behind while old Herb himself waddles along as well, losing ground with every step. A distant third. You press down on the accelerator and gun your Pontiac Aztek forward, back toward the center of town. With only one signal, a single traffic light, between you and the figurative border. The Switzerland of your dreams that lies just beyond the two blocks of business district that rushes past as you grip the wheel.

Los Feliz

◆

Tell me she's not fucking him. Just tell me that much.

That's all I can think in that first blur of handshake and forced smile. My handshake, his smile. He's already looking over my shoulder, looking to spot who he can meet next. See, we've had our moment; he's past me. And with her standing right next to him. Glowing. I mean, if I had to choose a word, describe her in a single phrase, it'd be "glowing." I'm not even gonna try to catch his eye again, see if we can start over, too late. Plus, I'm totally staring at her now, trying to work out this whole scenario for myself. Him and her. And are he and she doing the deed? Yeah, that *deed*. Please, God, someone tell me it isn't true! I mean, yes, why should I care? Fair enough, that is the question. Or, more appropriately, what right do I have to care? Me with a wife and 2.7 children at home, with the lovely house in Los Feliz and a pretty nice Lexus SUV out front (actually in the garage; you should never leave your vehicle out front in L.A., not even in Los Feliz). Who the hell am I that I should be caring if this woman is screwing that guy? I don't know, actually, who the hell I am, I just know that I care. For some reason I care. It bugs the shit out of me, in fact, if the truth be known. To be completely honest, it'd bother me to know that she's sleeping with anyone, but this guy in particular would really annoy me. Does annoy me. And I'm sure they are. Fucking, that is. It's just his way, that chummy way with her, the little smile and peck right on the lips that signals the whole damn thing to me, their history. God, I hate that! I mean, look at him, with the longish hair pulled back with a rubber band and hanging down the neck of his sport coat (when was that last "in"!?), the jeans and sandals, the IZOD shirt from, like, twenty years ago (with the big alligator, not the new little one), and the cigarette in one hand that he refuses to smoke. Just who in hell does he think he is? And now with the one hand on her neck, too. If I did that, I mean, in rehearsal or whatever, she'd look at me like I was nuts, well, not nuts but clearly on my way. If it wasn't in the script, I mean. If it's in the script then it's all right, it's open season. It says to giggle and she'll laugh out loud until the tears flow. It says "sex" and off come the clothes, even with only the stage crew in for a lineup. Not a problem. But try anything in the margin, off the page, after-hours, see where that gets you. I'm serious, try it. I have. And now this guy with the dull smile and the "yes, we first met in college" look as he massages her neck, brushes a finger over her ear. I love those ears! All right, no, I don't mean *love,* it can't be love because I've got the wife and the 2.7 kids and all the other shit I mentioned, but I'm very fond of those ears. I've grown quite attached to her ears over the two years we've spent on the series together and I don't like what I'm seeing here. Of course I don't say anything—are you crazy? I just nod and take my hand away as I mumble, "Nice to meet you," while I imagine impaling him on a pike or something fairly medieval. Bastard! And then he does the "whisper thing." He just leans over, like he's family now, leans over and says something to her. Making her laugh. I mean, fuck him! You know how many times I've tried to make that woman laugh? Do you?! Plenty, and it wasn't without a good deal of effort and at great personal cost. Not for lack of wanting, mind you, it's just that I'm not naturally funny. So, it's tough. But here comes ol' Lord Byron with the ponytail and a quip for every situation. And she eats it up. Just gobbles it down and drops to her knees, begging for more. Or at least smiles over at him. Which is plenty, believe me . . . have you ever seen one of her smiles? I mean a *real* smile, not one for the fans when we're out on tour, opening another shopping mall or electronics store, but one of those big, glorious ones that she saves for special occasions. Occasions like this, apparently. For a guy like that! Whom she must be giving head to, now that I see them together. The way she hangs on his arm. Glances back to see if he caught someone's name (as he checks out who he can meet next). The works! I know I should just finish my champagne and get my ass home to the wife and 2.7 kids; I mean, the Lexus is right out front with the valet, but I can't stop staring. I just snubbed one of the producers' wives—that's gonna cost me during salary negotiations, you can bet your ass on that—because I can't stop staring at the two of them. I'm starting to feel a bit homicidal now, which is frightening. Not frightening like I want to stop feeling this way, just that it's a party and there're too many witnesses around for a clean get-away. I honestly would like to kill the long-haired, gator-wearing motherfucker and would, I swear I would, if only the opportunity arose (and as long as I could be fairly certain there was no prison time involved). He's running a finger down her arm right now, look at that! Just tracing a lazy trail down the length of her bicep, a beautiful Coppertone bicep that he's got no business trailing down. And that's it. I can't take any more, so I don't. Just as their fingers are locking—she's talking to one of the costume designers, a lovely redhead with a talent for period detail, and he's ogling the new gal in casting, seriously, ogling her as he's holding hands with this angel from heaven!—I step forward and say something. Years from now I'll be able to blame it on the booze, when somebody bellows this story out at our one-hundredth-episode shindig or whenever, but right now I'm just hanging it all out there. I feel completely lucid and I'm telling you, I-just-can't-take-it-anymore. Total Howard Beale syndrome. You know, that one crazy dude from *Network*. So, I catch the guy's eyes, right, he's probably trying to see past me to another guest, but I hold his gaze long enough to say, quite eloquently, "Hey!" The room doesn't go silent, exactly, it's a big place after all, but the area around us definitely quiets down. Heads turning. She looks over at me, about to say something but I don't let her interfere, she's had her chance, plenty of chances as far as I'm concerned. She doesn't have to have a *relationship* with me, for God's sake, but does she have to drag this useless piece of sycophantic shit into a wrap party meant for us? For cast and crew? No, she doesn't, so I decide to say something. I say it, the "Hey" thing, and the guy looks at me, his lids heavy as the stone tablets that Moses carried down from on high, and he snorts out, "Yeah?" Now, there's my out. Right there. I could've said anything, or nothing, got my wits back together and just driven away to Los Feliz and it all would've been forgotten five minutes later. But no, I go ahead and say, "I mean, why don't you two just get a *room?*" Her face drops in sections, like snow falling from my parents' roof in February, as she whispers, "*What* did you say?" She starts to lean forward, but the guy slides in ahead of her, staring at me drunkenly as he pulls off—I gotta hand it to him—his coup de grace. He finally takes a long drag off that smoke of his, the one I mentioned, as he quite loudly states, "Well, we would bunk together if we were younger. But these days my *sister* and I like separate rooms . . ." You play these things back, let them zip back and forth in your head like flash cards, and you still don't see the clues. The same hairline. A pout in the mouth. The weight carried around the jaw. No, you just assume this is some asshole that she's fucking and you open your big, fat mouth. Why? Oh, because you want to fuck her, I suppose; it's that simple if you really break it down. Do the "analysis" shit. *You* desperately want to be the asshole on her arm that every other guy is jealously grumbling to himself about. Thinking, she can't possibly be fucking him, can she? I mean, not him!

I think this, all of this, as I stand in line now, waiting for the Lexus, my Lexus that will transport me back to Los Feliz and into the arms of my wife and 2.7 children, while noticing for the first time the crispness in the air on this late November night.

Some Do It Naturally

❖

Wait a second, I want you to hear this. Seriously, listen.
Those two, over there. Yeah, I know it's eavesdropping,
I know that, but you have to catch this; listen. It's not
wrong, come on, it's not illegal or anything, it's just not
that nice. Granted. Still, I can't help myself. Listen.

"... it's a life, I don't care what you say."

"I'm not saying that, who says I'm saying that? I
didn't."

"No, but you're implying it."

"I'm not either. I mean, not really."

"Ahh, yeah, you were ..."

"When? When did I say that?"

"Just now, with the 'if you do it soon it won't really matter' thing. Right there."

"I'm just saying scientifically. Scientists—you know, doctors or whoever—have argued for years that there's a certain cutoff point, like, a grace period or whatnot, before a thing becomes a person. Or a baby, or . . . you know what I'm saying."

"Yeah, I do, I know exactly what you're saying. You're making an argument for killing it."

"You don't kill something that's not alive."

"Now you're saying that it's not even . . ."

"I mean 'human,' that's all. With a soul and everything."

"But it does have, I believe that it has a . . ."

"I'm just repeating a theory."

"No, you're trying to make it OK. Make killing allowed."

"I'm not either, I promise I'm not. I'm only pointing out that people, people with a lot more degrees and learning and that sort of thing than us—I have a bachelor's, but that's no big deal—have agreed that life doesn't really take place until a certain point. That it's not instantaneous, that's all."

"How do you know that, though? Or them, even, how do they know for certain? I don't care if they studied at some big university or not, what do they know about the spirit of something?"

"Oh, brother."

"What?"

"Nothing. It's . . ."

"No, what? Go ahead."

". . . if you're gonna bring religion into it, then we might as well just forget it."

"Why?"

"Because it's messy. Religion is just a big mess when it comes to this stuff. Practical life stuff."

"I can't even believe you'd say that. What're you saying?"

"We shouldn't get off on some tangent here . . ."

"God isn't a 'tangent'! He means something, at least to me . . ."

"Yeah, really? What exactly?"

"He's . . . oh, don't do that. Make me explain. That's a lousy thing to do. He just isn't and religion is important, it's an important part of life, anyone would tell you that."

"Not anybody I know."

"Please. Sin, right and wrong, those kinds of things? That's all that really matters, when you actually get down to it. How we treat each other."

"Whatever. Look, if you wanna do this now—have some big biblical moment—then we can, but I don't think it's gonna help us make what is, in essence, a very practical decision."

"No, you're pushing me, you're pushing for an answer and I need to think about this. I do, I really need to just think . . ."

Come on, please, I'm not even listening in now—they're taking over the place with the volume they're speaking at. Look how everybody's staring at them. It's not just me. I mean, take it outside, right? Please. This is not what I come to lunch for, to listen to crap like this. I know, I know, then I shouldn't eavesdrop, but come on, they're classic, you have to admit. It really is amazing that people can get through life believing the stuff they do. It is to me, anyway. Oh, hold it, wait, wait, she's gonna say something else. Don't look at me like that; I'm not doing anything criminal. We're here, it's happening, I didn't plan it. *Shhh,* wait.

"... you know what the problem is?"

"What? Tell me."

"We're out of sync. Us two."

"Oh, please, come on. What does that even mean?"

"Step. Out of time, that kind of thing. We are not in rhythm with one another."

"No?"

"Uh-huh. No. We want different things . . ."

"Well, of course we want different things, of course we do . . . I mean, we're different people, aren't we? Two different people."

"Yes, but . . ."

"So that makes us distinct. Individual. And our wants, or desires—whatever you wanna call them—are going to be specific to who we are. Obviously. But that doesn't mean we can't long for similar kinds of things, or wish for our stuff to be in the ballpark of each other's, at least. Right?"

"Umm, I didn't actually follow that . . ."

"I'm just saying that, yes, you're not the same as me, or me you, but that doesn't make one of us right or wrong or better or anything. Or that we can't hope for some sort of synthesis between our disparate visions of life."

"That didn't actually help me. I mean, I was with you for most of it, as you were speaking, but when you use words like that, like . . ."

"Look, I'm saying that we're compatible, you and I are. We are. Just because we see this baby situation from two sides doesn't mean that . . ."

"No, but, see, that's the point for me. Right there. That there aren't two sides to it."

"There're two sides to anything. Come on, don't tell me that . . ."

"Uh-uh. I don't feel that way. Not about this."

"But . . ."

"Not about a life, no. A human life."

"All right, listen, we're going in circles here, because we're basically back to the science and religion crap and now we're just going to get angry."

"I already am, I mean, kind of."

"Why? What'd I do, except try to explain that we're . . ."

"I just don't want to discuss this, really. Maybe that's it."

"Well, that's too bad, OK? Too bad for you because we need to. This has got to be looked at, examined, since there are two people involved. And, obviously, two very unique philosophies at play."

"I'm not one of your college buddies, OK, so you don't have to impress me with your word choices . . ."

"What word, where?"

"'Philosophies' and all that."

"That is not a big word."

"No, I know, but you don't really have to use it, either. You could just be direct and truthful with me here."

"I am being truthful. I don't want this kid, how's that? Pretty naked statement right there."

"Fine."

"'Fine' what? Fine, you understand, or fine, you'll do what I'm asking?"

"I get it. I won't do that, what you want, but I follow what you're saying . . ."

Don't pull on my arm like that! All right? Just don't. You are not the conversation police here, so far as I'm aware. I am not breaking the law or anything, peeking over into my neighbor's yard or that kind of deal . . . these two are going at it right in front of us, and I, for one, find it pretty damn interesting. And you know what? Look around, seriously, take a quick glance, and you'll see that I'm not the only one. Everybody in the joint is gawking at them. Seriously, look. That woman right there—if you'd turn your head for a second you'd see her—in the orange blouse, no, behind the palm frond, yes. Her. See? Her fork is hovering at her mouth, been that way for, like, ten minutes. So, you know, whatever. Don't listen, then, go wait in the car if I'm such an embarrassment, I'll get the check. When don't I get the check, anyway? It won't come as a shock . . . I'm sorry, but it's not a flaw in my nature, my character or whatnot, because I'm curious to see how the other half lives. You know I'm like that. Yes, I am. I'm always coming home and saying, "Hold on, I need to write this down before I forget it," and that sort of thing. "You'll never believe what so-and-so said." People surprise me, constantly surprise and delight me, and I can't help it. Wait, now they're talking about sex. Hold on.

"... then you should've had them on hand. I mean, if you want me to use 'em that badly."

"That is so rotten to say."

"What?"

"That it's my problem . . ."

"I'm not saying that it's a problem, I'm only stating that—as a fact—if you want something to happen, then you're usually better off if you make it happen. Be pro-active or whatever, instead of just hoping for the best."

"I asked you to wait . . ."

"I don't remember that."

"I did! I said to please run down to the drugstore on the corner and get some and you wouldn't, so I said then can we just mess around, not go all out if that was the case. I did say that, I completely remember it."

"It was late."

"I know."

"It was late and cold, too, I think."

"Yes, but . . ."

"And so then it becomes my responsibility, right?"

"Well . . . yeah, basically."

"Why? Why is that?"

"Because . . ."

"Yes?"

"It's . . . since it's for your . . . thing."

"So?"

"So you should provide for it, then, I guess."

"That's quite a theory you've got there . . . Freud's got nothing on you."

"Don't do that. OK? Don't bully me and make me feel stupid."

"I'm not, I promise you, I'm not doing that. It's just that, I dunno, you're making me feel bad about this and I don't think that's right . . . you're pregnant. We have a situation here and you wanna tie it all up in these arguments that are getting us nowhere."

"All I said was you should've brought a condom . . ."

"But I don't like them."

"Yeah, but you don't like a baby either, now, do ya?"

"No. No, I'm . . . I mean, not at this time."

"So . . ."

"Why would I do that, though, carry them . . . if I hate the way they feel?"

"To avoid crap like this. To keep from sitting in a restaurant and talking about our whole lives in front of a bunch of strangers. Maybe for a reason like that."

"Oh, please, don't be so . . . nobody's listening to us."

"No?"

"God, no. People have their own shit to worry about."

"I feel like everyone's staring . . ."

"Not at all. A girl getting herself knocked up doesn't have the same allure it did a decade or so ago. Believe me. You're not Tess of the D'Urbervilles."

"Who?"

"Just this girl . . . in a book. Nothing."

"I didn't do that."

"What?"

"Get myself knocked up, all right? Don't talk like that, because it makes me feel . . ."

"I was just . . ."

". . . it makes me sick."

"Sorry. I didn't mean that, it's just an expression. I meant us. We did."

"All right then. Anyway, all I'm saying is . . ."

I can feel you looking at me, OK? I don't even have to turn around to know that you're doing it. I sense the heat coming off your eyes. You're like something out of a science fiction film, with laser beams shooting out. You're only making yourself look silly now, so do what you want. I'm not going yet. Listen, how many stores did I have to wander through this afternoon, huh? How many? I know it's not the same thing, not the exact same thing but I'm just pointing out to you that I did that, dutifully walked along there next to you and said how nice you looked and carried the bags and dug around on the

shelves for the match to those shoes and I didn't say a
thing. Not a goddamn thing the whole time. Even this
place was your idea, remember? I just wanted a sandwich. So if I happen to stumble onto a little pleasure
for five seconds, to find something that grabs my fancy
during the middle of a long Sunday, I don't know why
on earth that should bother you at all. Not one tiny bit.
He's paying their check now, paying the bill, so they're
just about through. I'll be outside in five minutes, so go
have the valet pull the car around. I'll be there in . . .
less than that; I'm three minutes away. Please just do
it, don't give me the turned-up eyes or the "big sigh"
shit because I just might scream if you do. Scream like
a little schoolgirl if I hear one more of those puffs of
displeasure slip out of that mouth of yours. Just go. Oh,
see, now I missed something, because of you. There
now, he's . . . look. Look at that.

    ". . . I don't wanna fight with you."
    "I don't either."
    "You know I don't like it and it makes me feel
sad."
    "Me, too."

"I know, so let's . . ."

"Fine."

"We can talk more about it at home. Later or some-thing."

"That's good."

"I feel like . . ."

Why do you have to make this about us? Huh? Turn some petty argument between two kids into some grand epi-sode ripped from the pages of our life together? You are so self-consumed, you know that? You are. I don't think I've ever even used those words before and here I am, saying them about my own wife. You are obsessed with you. My God, this has nothing to do with us not having children . . . I can't believe that you'd even, Jesus. You're impossible. You really are, or you've gotten that way over the last few years. Maybe that's it. You dazzled me with your looks and that smile and the way that you entertain when a friend drops by . . . something. Something has kept me from realizing the kind of person you are. I mean, seriously, to even say that, to bring up our . . . don't stand up now. Don't do that, make some scene out of this. Please don't. Well, fine, but I'm turning around, I'm going to turn and watch those two leave because that's interesting to me, their story holds some mystery and intrigue to anyone watching, whereas you're just making a spectacle of yourself. A pathetic middle-aged spectacle. See, now he's got his back to me. Damn it! I can't hear what he's saying.

". . . and you still feel that way, then we'll make a decision."

"OK."

"All right?"

"Yeah. That seems fair."

"Anyway, I'm sorry. I am."

"Me too. I'm . . . did you leave enough?"

"I think. I think so . . . seven dollars is good, right?"

"Probably."

Well, I missed it. The finale of it happened and I missed it, thanks to you. I don't even know if you're still there, because I'm not turning around yet. Not quite yet. And if you ask yourself why, if there's room there inside your head for any thought that doesn't have specifically to do with you . . . I'm not turning around because you sicken me. That's why. You piss me off and treat me so badly that I've just about had all that I can take. OK? This is a declaration of war, I guess, because I have had my fill. My absolute fill of your shit and your ways. And it comes so naturally to you, that's what really frightens me. Your ability to hurt and mistreat me, it's like a part of your makeup. Your very fiber. I bet you're there, I'm sure you are, you wouldn't miss a thing like this for the world. This moment. Some second where everyone in the place is twisted around in their seats to see what the hell's going on under our umbrella. With your sunglasses and piled-up hair and a tan you bought with a coupon book. That's you. That is my wife and welcome to her. What was it that comedian used to say, that fellow with all the—he'd come onstage and do the wife jokes. Remember? "Take my wife. Please." Those jokes, that's what you've become to me. A punch line. A mockery of the woman I loved and wedded and slipped off to Venice with in my youth. You are not her. She was swallowed up long ago, devoured by the thing you've become. Like one of those monster pictures that I went to as a kid, those Saturday double bills that my parents scooted me off to with friends. You are some fifty-foot woman or two-headed beast that no longer even resembles the woman of my dreams, so I refuse to look at you. I do. And you want to know why? Huh? Because I don't want to be turned to stone, into a pillar of stone by your Medusa-like stare, that's why. I'm going to sit here all day and pray that when I swivel back around you'll be gone. Gone with the car and into a ditch, returned to the womb of that hell from which you crawled. That is my wish. My dream. My desire. Go away now. Go on. Go.

Grand Slam

◈

If she opens her mouth again, I'm gonna fucking kill her. I am.

I catch myself saying this, not out loud or anything, God no, but absolutely thinking it, you know, there inside my head, as I'm smiling across the table at her and nodding. Nodding for, like, the *hundredth* time as she rambles on about her mother and growing up in Wisconsin and the most inane shit I've ever heard come out of a person's mouth. She's been going at it, this talking stuff, I mean, for around three hours straight, seriously, without a pause, and it's really getting me down. I almost feel sad inside, or lonely or something, because of it. Which is a weird feeling. To be with somebody, sitting across from them, and at the same time having a moment where it's like you are so completely and utterly by yourself that you wanna scream or weep or some emotion like that. Kind of like that one picture of the dude clutching the sides of his head and crying out—you know the one I'm talking about? It's famous, I think. My high school English teacher had it hanging in her class—I don't know the name of the guy who painted it—and I used to stare at it a lot, especially during tests. Anyway, I'm sorta like that right now. Her talking is making me feel that way and I don't like it. Not that I enjoy having these other thoughts, the ones about pounding her goddamn head in with a brick or a chunk of concrete or something. I don't really want to have urges like these toward a person, any person at all, so it's depressing to be driven to a place like that. Some kind of murderous place all because the bitch can't shut her fucking mouth.

I didn't even want to go out with her in the first place, not that this is a date, what we're doing right now. Not an official one, anyway, the kind you'd call a romance if you were talking about it with friends. It's not that. She talked me into having a meal because I was hungry and said OK and that's how I find myself here, but it's not a date. I want to be clear about that. This is not the kind of woman I want to be out with, spending my time on, and things like that. I'm not attracted to her, don't even want to be *seen* with her, really, but she lives two floors down from me and I figured food is food and so I said, "Fine, let's eat," and now I'm living to regret it. She's like some fucking *infomercial* that you wake up to at four in the morning because you fell asleep watching *All in the Family;* the thing is just going on and on and you know you can't really place small ads in hundreds of newspapers and make any money but you keep listening anyway. I find her very much like that. Hell, I'd even pay the five easy payments of $19.95 if this beast would quit sucking down Diet Coke and pay the check and drive me the fuck back to my apartment. We've been done eating for maybe forty-five minutes—did a piece of cheesecake, even— and she's showing no signs of letting up. It really is unbeliev-able. She is definitely on a tear. I mean, *Milwaukee!* What the fuck else can you say about that place? I bet if Jef-frey Dahmer had known about this chick, he would've eased off on the little boys for a second and done the world a favor, throttled this twat, and diced her up into little bite-size chunks. Now, I know that's not very nice, not a Christian-type thing to say, and I wasn't raised like that but that's how I'm starting to feel here, trapped in our little booth and nodding my head and hoping to God somebody robs the place and she gets caught in the police crossfire. I know I shouldn't let my thoughts spill over into such mean-spirited shit as that, but believe me, if you were sitting where I am, you'd be reaching for the chainsaw right now. I promise you would.

I'm thinking about ordering myself a second Grand Slam as she launches into another long rant about her mom. I mean, what the hell, why not? If this is the way she's gonna play it, promise me anything off the menu and then practically hold me captive at the Denny's for the better part of an evening, then I should at least get something out of the deal. Slams're on sale, anyway, not like she's gonna be out a bundle because of it. Not at all. I put my hand up in the air for the waitress while holding eye contact. I mean, I'd like to look away, check out the whole staff because the girls in here are pretty cute— that one with the hair dyed candy-apple red especially— but I'd better not because she'd notice a thing like that, this gal would, notice it right off and probably say something about it. And not just something, either, but a twenty-minute riff on me and guys in general and us being like animals in the field and never opening up or being worth her time and some big essay on the current state of mankind, and so I figure, Fuck that, I'll just signal with a finger and keep listening to this fat sow go on about her mom's failing eyesight and the like. I'm so close to grabbing the syrup container or the bottle of ketchup there and just going to town on her fucking skull that I don't know what, but I'm trying my best to keep it together. I don't honestly think a court in this great country of ours would convict me, but you can't just go around whacking the shit out of people. That's what my mom used to say, anyhow, and I'm doing what I can to live by it. It's fucking hard, though, lemme tell you. Right now, especially.

The redhead notices my distress call and waltzes over to see what all the commotion's about. It's not really a commotion or anything; I mean, I'm not doing shit, just sitting there, but this woman I'm with is not just talking and talking and talking but is waving her hands in the air as she goes and moving those fingers of hers in all directions to emphasize every fucking noun and verb. A cigarette sucked straight down to the filter in one ring-filled claw. I glance over at this gal as she arrives, the cute one in the uniform, and even toss her a little half smile, just so she knows I'm

sitting here but in no way am I with this loud-mouth whore.
Not at all. I think she gets the idea, what with me making
sure that she sees I've got no ring on my finger and I'm
plenty interested in her but my plate is kinda full at the
moment. So I order up the Slam, actually go with the All-
American this time around, just to mix it up a little, and
she nods—name is "Missy"—and walks off the long way,
back the other direction so I can grab a quick shot of her
ass when she rounds the corner up toward the counter.
And no letup from this one across the way; I mean, like,
not even a goddamn *breath* the whole time. My "date" hits
about three dozen topics during the quick exchange with
the Denny's gal and shows no sign of slowing. Talks about
Medicare and how hard it is to cash a Social Security check
without ID and that Safeway has got a sale going on Hungry Man TV dinners and how much she detests meeting
guys on the Internet but she's really, really horny and suddenly I'm thinking the extra food may be a bad idea. Did
she just say "horny"? Oh come on, I'm gonna throw up, I
swear to Christ, if she gets into the personal stuff. I mean,
you know, it's one thing to go get a bite and chitchat and
things of that nature, but I'm gonna just barf right here in
her lap if she starts talking about getting laid. I really, really will. And I don't give a damn who sees me, either.

Luckily, the Slam arrives to save me a couple minutes later, but the damage is already done. Ol' Chatty Kathy has charted her course, laid her cards on the table, and any other fucking expressions you can come up with. That's why we're here. That's how come all the nice crap in the lobby and holding the door for me and that type of deal the last few months. The bitch wants some sort of sexual shit from me. Jesus, if that isn't always the way. Worst part is—well, not really *worse* than the idea of touching this big, sloppy lush but very close—the redhaired gal catches part of the conversation when she comes back with my hash browns. Right as she's leaning over me—and I mean *way* in close, her name tag practically catching on my upper lip—the downstairs-from-me chick starts raving about the ins and outs of giving head, about how much she digs it and craves it and all this kind of thing—like how she is so great at it and can't wait to be doing it again and all that—but this waitress doesn't understand that it's only talk so she just looks at me, this maybe twenty-two-year-old cutie does, tosses a big "it's your loss, buddy" look my way and off she goes. The other route this time, back where I can't see her. So now that's dead. No chance, thanks to little Miss Blow Job here, and that's that. Fuck. Great. That's really great.

Point being, make a long story short and whatnot, all
that other shit I just mentioned—the Denny's Grand
Slam shit—is how I find myself back here at the apartment complex, standing in some cramped back bedroom
at nine o'clock in the P.M. and missing the game while this
lady slobbers away on my dick. Both hands clamped
around my ass. Nails digging in. I can hear the TV in the
other room, already the sixth inning or something like
that—Cubbies are down 4–0 now because somebody hit
one out—but I am totally missing it. The game. I look
around the place, this "guest room" that she's done up in
animal posters and throw pillows and stuff of that nature,
and try to trace back just how the fuck I got here, to this
very moment. It's almost like I'm there, you know, there
in her place but removed from it, too, some kind of out-
of-body thing that you might hear about in the *Reader's
Digest.* I see her down there in front of me, sitting forward on the edge of the floral comforter and going at it—
she didn't lie, she's not half bad at this—and I'm staring
at all those dark roots growing out of her scalp and I find
that I'm thinking these thoughts and, I swear to Christ,
catch myself tearing up. Seriously, starting to tear up a
little bit in the, like, half-light of this chick's apartment.
I mean, what the fuck? I notice this, this very surprising

shit that's happening to me, and I suddenly wanna push her away, toss her back on the bed, and pull up my Wranglers and run the hell outta there, up the stairs to my living room, and sit on my sofa and watch the game, maybe just be alone for a second. But I don't. I do not do that. What I do is I keep standing there, legs spread a bit and checking out some torn picture of a bison that she's pushpinned up over her bamboo headboard. I notice it, this big shaggy fucker glaring over at me, and I can't take my eyes off it. I can't. And I guess, basically, that's all there is. The sound of her going at it down there, the television in the distance. And this buffalo. Looking out at me and me looking at him. Not blinking, just staring straight ahead. Both of us. Quiet.

Whitecap

◆

I guess it's about at twenty thousand feet when I first spot her. Right around there. Twenty, maybe twenty-five. Not cruising altitude; I don't think we're there yet, because the seatbelt sign hasn't gone off, so we must be climbing still. Yes, I'm sure we are. Climbing. Plus, the weather isn't great. I'm working in first this flight, which is odd, anyway, because I usually don't. I mean, I have a few times, short hops from, like, Chicago to Atlanta or wherever, some training when I started, but not since I've switched to the "international" thing. Not on this route yet. But we need someone else up front because we're pretty full, you know, lots of people coming over for Wimbledon or who knows what, summer break, I guess. So, I'm starting to pour out OJs and ginger ales and whatnot, just getting us ready. Cups of water. Mixed nuts. And I spot her.

She's up in the bulkhead seats, here in the front, and I'm staring her right in the eye, maybe ten feet away, off to the left. Like, 1H and K. K, the window, for her son (about six, I suppose), and she's in H, the aisle, with this baby in her arms. A baby. Yeah. I've been going out with the guy for eighteen months, I mean, basically *living* with him, you know, and I don't know anything about this infant. Do you believe that? See, he spends two weeks a month in England, her husband, some company he works for, and I'm based out of there now, too. In London. We met on this flight, in fact, when I was moving my things over.

I recognize her from a picture I'd seen in his billfold once. He'd jammed it down in one of those little side pockets, the kind for change or keys, folded twice and shoved inside there. It was an older-type snapshot, the kind with the white borders, and was tucked inside a receipt. It was color, a sort of candid thing from her youth, playing sports or on vacation or something. There

was water, too, I guess, in the background, so maybe at
the ocean. She had a visor on, in the photo, but I knew
who she was immediately when I saw her there. In 1H.
Anyway, he'd hidden the thing away. I don't know why.
Maybe so I wouldn't find it, maybe because he didn't
want to think about her right then. Not sure, really. But
I saw it once when he was showering and our Thai food
showed up and I needed a few extra pounds or something to pay for it . . . so that's how I know it's her. Sitting in that aisle seat.

She's pretty. A little heavy, maybe, but pretty. She's
sitting there, all tired and the boy crawling on her and
the baby whimpering, and she's waving to me. Wants me
to heat up some formula for her or something. So, I
gather myself, I do, I gather myself up and go over and
turn off her little blinking light overhead and I say, "Hi,
can I help you?" She fires off a series of instructions in
response, then sends me away with a wave of her mater-
nal hand. Looking up only long enough to read my name.
"Robin." I see her saying it to herself, mouthing it as she
lets the baby squeeze her finger. "Robin."

When I come back to her with the bottle, I casually
ask where they're headed and she tosses off a quick answer, with a voice deeper than I expect, saying she and

the kids are using some frequent-flier miles to go to the UK. Surprise "Daddy" for his birthday. And as she smiles thinly at me, the dismissive smile of someone who no longer requires my service, I envision her at Heathrow struggling through customs with the children and her bags and fighting for a cab and winding through the serpentine streets of Mayfair and looking for his address and the surprise on both their faces when she is greeted at the door by him wearing my robe. Incense in the air. Two of my pressed uniforms still hanging in the bathroom archway.

At that moment, the sun breaks through some clouds and pours in a nearby window, engulfing her. Backlit now, the years drop away from her face. I think of this woman from another time, that captive image in her husband's wallet—young and hopeful and dressed for the beach—but the light soon fades and as I return to pouring drinks and handing out menus, I too smile thinly, knowing that life will never be the same for her again.

Soft Target

◆

This was going to be one of those days; he could feel it. Not an ordinary one, oh no, this was one of those that crept up on him—starting at around 10:30 or so—and made a bit of a fuss for the rest of the morning-slash-afternoon. This was going to be just like that.

It had started off well enough, with a nice call from his mother—well, not *nice* exactly, but short—and then a quick jog up the canyon. Runyon wasn't the prettiest of walks or the most invigorating, but there were a lot of people with dogs who used those trails and that usually meant a fair number of girls. Or "women"—whatever. He was so tired of trying to figure out who went by what and at what age you could still call someone a "girl" or when you had to say "'woman" that he no longer bothered. And names were impossible. Absolutely impossible. No, the best thing to do, he reasoned, was to just pitch right in when he bumped into someone that he even vaguely recognized and say, "Hey, how's it going?" with a big smile-slash-grin, making it seem like the two of them were past having to play any of those introductory games anymore. Well past. And he wasn't more than thirty yards up the path—not even to the gate where you can unleash your animals—when he got the chance to put his little theory to work.

She was someone from a while ago—maybe around February—one of those girls-slash-women whom he had immediately singled out as a definite maybe and then gone in for the kill. She was an actress-slash-model—of course—and had only been in town for about two years. Maybe even less. This was the perfect kind of girl-slash-woman, he always felt, because she was still hopeful, still had a bit of bounce left in her, but had also experienced just enough of the rejection and longing and money troubles that she was also extremely vulnerable. Very. In fact, open to just about anything. He'd liked her right off—practically right off, after the first time they slept together, anyway—and had met her not half a mile from here, actually, up on the north ridge of the park as she was finishing off a bottle of Evian. He'd spotted her and made a snide comment about the French, which got them both laughing. The French were an easy target with actresses because—although they all secretly wished that they were Catherine Deneuve—none of those French starlets had ever really made it big in Hollywood and that's what actually mattered to American actresses. So he'd made the French crack—something about her looking like the girl-slash-woman in *Manon of the Spring* or that kind of thing—and they'd shared a smile and a walk back down the hill. A fairly leisurely walk, too, with no real pretense of exercise taking place. He'd even given her a lift home that day, since her car—an '82 white Toyota, which fairly screamed that she had very little cash—wouldn't start when they reached the lower parking area. He fiddled with a few wires under the hood to make it look good—he actually hated cars and knew next to nothing about them—but he knew fully well that it was going to be a ride back in the '04 BMW that she really needed. And that's exactly what he was going to give her. A ride. A ride and then some.

On the way to her apartment—some barely decent complex down around Wilshire, just off Detroit—he fiddled with the CD player–slash–stereo while asking her a rash of seemingly simple questions but ones that he had actually perfected from a number of previous attempts. There was no specific order to them, but each was designed to accomplish two general things: put the girl-slash-woman at ease and give him a basic understanding of what her position in the creative community was. By question 3 they'd decided to swing past his place first, and it didn't take more than five answers—well, after the "Where you from?" and "Oh, sure, I've been there!" give-and-take—before he knew without a doubt that she was a keeper. Now, by "keeper" he didn't mean that this was the girl-slash-woman of his dreams or anything silly like that, oh no, but just that she was easily someone who was worth being around for a bit, having some fun with, and then getting rid of when it was time to get serious about hooking up with somebody for the summer. See, the "summer" girl-slash-woman was always a big deal and not to be taken lightly. No, this one here was nothing more than a soft target and he knew it. Hell, even she probably knew it and it didn't seem to bother her. Not one tiny bit.

They'd slept together that first day, even—which is a gentle way of saying that she had given him head in his garage and he'd spent most of the afternoon fucking her from behind while the gardener was trimming the hedges—and so he decided to throw her a bone and invite her out to lunch-slash-dinner. Some nice spot on Melrose, he reasoned—one of those Italian ones—which would make her happy to be seen at but was actually a year or so out of the loop. This way, if he were to run into somebody that he knew—or, even worse, mattered—then he could laugh it off rather than have to explain himself or worry about some picture showing up in *People* magazine or the like. Some days he wished dinner was a little easier to manage, rather than the elaborate shell game that it often turned out to be. It was also unthinkable to have to go through the whole dance of taking her home, then coming back to the house for a few hours while she got dolled up, and then having to go back to her place again later and meet her friend-slash-roommate, who would go on and on about how much she loved his films (this happened almost every time he dated an aspiring actress and every time he dated a "civilian," so this wasn't some pathetic, elevated sense of self; he was simply being realistic), and then driving her over to the restaurant. Instead, he suggested that they go down and park a bit early—she insisted that she couldn't go out looking like she did, in her workout stuff—and he'd buy her something new, a nice new outfit, which could be a lot of fun. For her, at least. Her eyes lit up when she heard that one, the idea of going shopping and having dinner all in one fell swoop. This was going to be just like hanging out at the mall with her girlfriends back in Kansas— she was literally from Kansas, no joke—except that she'd be having sex again later, which is probably not how her shopping sprees at home in Overland Park usually ended. Although who knows? People are funny.

So they'd done the shopping—she bought a couple of those vintage T-shirts that the kids are so crazy for these days and a nice little skirt and a pair of pink Pumas—and had the dinner—made it all the way through coffee-slash-dessert without seeing anyone he knew, thank God—and then, as expected, headed back over to his house. His home was tucked away in a fashionable part of the hills, not up off Sunset but a touch farther down, closer to

Griffith Park. She jumped out of his car right when they got there, didn't even wait for him to get the door but acted like she owned the place. Smiled over at him as he fished for his keys, and put on that "I'm so used to this lifestyle already" face that he'd seen a dozen times before on girls-slash-women and had hated each time. Who was she kidding? She'd probably never even cleaned a house this size, let alone had the run of the joint. Oh well. Let her have her fun. Twenty minutes later they were in the pool, naked and drinking martinis out of big plastic glasses that he'd picked up from a publicity person on one of his junkets. They had liquid trapped inside them and the name of a film he'd done last summer emblazoned across them in cherry red. She really did have a nice body, this girl-slash-woman—the walking up and down that canyon had to be good for something—and she wasn't exactly shy about showing herself off, which was one nice thing. She had an exceptional ass, one of those storybook cans that make men spend good money on cheap magazines. Perfect shape and as taut as fine material stretched over a wooden frame. Lovely. Her breasts—he never called them "tits" unless they'd been augmented by surgery;

it was a personal quirk of his—were OK, but just that. Nothing to write home about, even if you were already in the middle of a letter. They were big enough, just about right, actually, but one seemed to be a touch larger than the other and the nipples bothered him a bit. Here in the pool they were fine, but when they were relaxed—"at bay," he liked to say to himself—the nipples were inverted and that was something that creeped him out. There were just these sort of slits where the tips would normally be and no way of coaxing them out unless the girl-slash-woman got excited about something. That didn't seem normal. Bobbing up and down in the water, though, he forgot about that and just enjoyed the feeling of her rubbing up against him as they listened to the crickets and watched a couple of spotlights trace lazy lines across the evening sky. Somewhere down in town was a premiere-slash-gala that he hadn't been invited to—heads would roll tomorrow for that one—and people were running around seeing movies or going to parties or having dinner. But instead of being a part of all that, that normal progression of the night, he had a naked girl-slash-woman in his pool and she had her hand wrapped firmly around his cock-slash-balls. It was a moment like this—not the awards shows or the photo shoots of an interview with Barbara Walters—that made him feel different from everyone else. He turned away from the view and decided to let her get down to it, as it were, splashing some water on her nipples to jumpstart the proceedings.

And here she was again, that girl-slash-woman from a few months ago, coming down the path. He hadn't really called her or anything after that initial meeting—he gave her a number, of course, but it was to his agent-slash-manager and after a few weeks she'd stopped ringing—so this was probably going to be a bit awkward. There were a couple of options, of course, and they all seemed to run through his mind simultaneously:

1. ACT LIKE YOU DON'T KNOW HER. Now, this was probably the lamest and most desperate of the possibilities, but he gave it a quick mulling over. In this scenario, he wouldn't avert his eyes or look the other way—pretending that his nonexistent dog had run down the hill or something, which he had resorted to on occasion—or turn around and start jogging in the other direction. Oh no, that would be way too much work for a girl-slash-woman like this. In this case, he'd simply keep going and make eye contact and see if she remembered

him. He had the sun to his back so it was possible that she wouldn't be able to make him out clearly, but he couldn't rely on that. If she did look at him—smiling or scowling or seething—he'd have to play dumb through to the end. Rarely would anyone actually stop and confront him; no, this approach usually only led to a dirty look or a whispered curse to a friend-slash-acquaintance as the girl-slash-woman in question walked off. No big deal. So, all in all, this was actually a pretty decent option and not nearly as lame or desperate as he had first felt it to be.

2. ACKNOWLEDGE HER BUT KEEP IT LIGHT. This one was obviously a touch harder to pull off and took a deeper commitment to the situation than perhaps he was willing to make at this time. In this sequence, he would make contact first and give a friendly wave-slash-smile, thereby rendering her attack mute. He wouldn't call her by name—he couldn't swear that she had ever told it to him in the first place—but utilize his earlier theory by pitching right in with a "Hi!" or "How's it going?" They could then make some light chatter-slash-banter about the weather and a few auditions that she'd gone on and didn't get, that sort of thing, until he

casually dropped in a yawn and said, "Well, hey, I better get going." This was tricky, of course, because the worst case was that she might ask him what he was doing over the weekend or did he need her number or something, but he'd seen this used very effectively by himself and others in the right situation. Usually with the more passive kinds of girls-slash-women, of which she seemed right on the cusp of being.

3. PICK UP RIGHT WHERE YOU LEFT OFF WITH HER. Actually a finesse move, but excellent at throwing a girl-slash-woman off. Or "for a loop," as one of the Teamsters on his latest picture was fond of saying when somebody screwed up the shooting schedule. In making this work, however, a physical element was often required, and he just wasn't sure he was up to it. He would need to really sell the "Hey there!" part of it, and then immediately follow up with a big hug—like how he'd behave if he ran into somebody that he had done television with years ago. With her it would be easy enough since he remembered a few details about her—the shopping, going to Angeli for dinner, etc.—but this strategy could get very dicey if he had no real sense of how or where or even why he'd spent time with someone.

This might be the right choice in this particular case, he
mused, but he decided to run through the rest of his
favorites, just to be sure.

4. BUTTER HER UP WITH A FALSE SENSE OF
    HOPE. Really a variation on a theme, since this called
    for something very similar to idea number 3, with a few
    slight but telltale changes. He would still need to
    execute the recognition-slash-hug-slash-personalization
    part of the routine, but then take it a step further by
    accepting nothing less than another date (time and
    place to be finalized right on the spot). Take her
    number this time—she'd be wary of the old office
    phone gag by this point—and set up a definite time to
    speak about going to a movie, or even better, a play, or
    a museum-slash-gallery. Most girls-slash-women, when
    they hear "play" or "museum," get quite excited and
    figure this is it, things are finally turning around for
    good. Now he's getting serious. Theater, by and large,
    was shit in Los Angeles—only because people use it as
    a stepping stone for getting a series-slash-film—but it
    was miraculous what it did for a girl-slash-woman when
    he offered to pick up some tickets and make a big night
    of it. He hardly ever used this one since it was so damn

concrete, and a girl-slash-woman like this would probably never force him into a situation that necessitated it, so it was a fair bet that this notion would be quickly thought about and discarded as she was approaching. Still, it had its charms.

5. ASK HER TO VISIT YOU ON THE SET. And here was the real granddaddy of them all—the public acknowledgment-slash-acceptance of her in front of his peers. Frankly, this girl-slash-woman didn't seem like a candidate for this one, but he had to give all his greatest hits a whirl before she reached him. If he were to use this one, he would do most of the positive things that he'd already listed above, but then up the ante by inviting her out to Warner Brothers, where he was shooting a thriller-slash-romance with that one girl from the college comedy that did really well last summer. If he had to sweeten the deal—like, if she was spitting mad—he might even promise her a speaking role in the film, which was enough to de-escalate practically any actress he had ever met. And besides, the road from speaking role to "featured extra" was really a simple journey—have her show up on a day that he's not working and have his assistant deal with all the fallout

and disappointment. If she stays around after that—a big
if—then send her to wardrobe and have the assistant
director—whom he'd gone to college with and who is
always ready to help out a friend—use her in that crowd
scene that they've planned for the late afternoon. This
notion was actually fairly generous—she would get paid
for the day—and it wouldn't cost him a thing, even
though by the end of the shooting day everybody would
know exactly who she was and that could be deadly,
especially if he were dating someone else or scoping out
some other girl-slash-woman already working on the
film. That's why this one—as easy to pull off as it
appeared—held the vaunted last-ditch spot in his "what
to do in case of emergencies with girls-slash-women" list.

By the time she reached him he had decided to go with
number 4, to be proactive in the moment and ask her
out again. Hell, why not? She did have that butt and he
didn't have to look at her breasts if he didn't want to and
she had been pretty flirty and eager and fun to have
around that day. So, then, why not, indeed? They could
probably still catch an afternoon film over at the Sunset Five or at one of those new places with the multiple
screens and stores and crap all around—there was a new

Iranian film out that he thought sounded kind of good—and then maybe order in some food later. Go for a swim-slash-jacuzzi. See what happens. Of course he knew what would happen, the same as before, only a little less spontaneous and a little less thrilling. But that's all right, he thought, that's not terrible for a Tuesday. In fact, this could end up being a terrific little Tuesday, much better than he'd imagined when he was parking his car and walking up those first switchbacks to the trail he was now on.

He realized almost immediately that she didn't see him as she passed—again, maybe it was the sun or something—and normally he would've said something, a good line thrown back over his shoulder about her hair or her outfit, then jogged down to speak with her. But not this time. Oh no, not today because she was already with someone. She was walking along and chatting up this guy he knew—well, he'd seen all of his movies—this writer-slash-director that he'd been interested in working with for some time now. This guy had had a semihit over in Europe—at Cannes or Venice or one of those, had won a Golden something—and had also made a big, silly action-slash-buddy-slash-road picture for Paramount-slash-Miramax that had somehow sparked at the box

office and done a hundred million or so. Maybe more
(twice that on video and DVD). In other words, he was
doing just fine, thank you, and here he was, totally out of
place up in the canyon with his Prada alpine garb on, but
talking to this girl-slash-woman in short little staccato
whispers that made her smile. She'd been smiling, in
fact—almost laughing, really—when they'd passed and
that's how she'd missed him. The two men actually made
eye contact, recognizing each other from publicity stills
or magazine articles, and the European fellow glanced
back for a moment. The two artists locked eyes in silence,
but then on they both went in their respective directions—the writer-slash-director still whispering to this
actress as they disappeared down an incline. The irony
of this—this girl-slash-woman incident—was not lost on
him and he laughed to himself at the absurdity of his
thoughts, his career, his life. He looked back one last
time—really only hoping for a final ass shot—then turned
around to face the rest of the climb while keeping an eye
out for dogs and their owners. After all, summer was
nearly here. It was time to get serious.

   He smiled and surged upward, thinking of all the possibilities that a city like this—spread out behind him like

a children's pop-up book—had to offer. Maybe this year
I'll go with a black one, he thought to himself. Or even
an Asian. He wasn't sure, of course, but he was open to
the day and what might lie ahead. Ahead up there somewhere, just around the bend-slash-corner.

Acknowledgments

◆

My name alone on the title page belies the efforts of a number of terrific people whose encouragement, craft, and inspiration made this book possible. You know who you are and I thank you all.

First published in the United States in 2004
By Grove/Atlantic, Inc.
Grove Press
841 Broadway
New York, NY 10003

First published in the United Kingdom in 2004
by Faber and Faber Limited
3 Queen Square London WC1N 3AU
This paperback edition first published in 2005

Printed in England by Mackays of Chatham plc, Chatham, Kent

Some of the stories in this collection have appeared in the following
publications, sometimes in slightly different form: "Maraschino" in *Black
Book*; "Time-Share" in *British Esquire*; "Grand Slam" in *British Esquire*
and Nerve.com; "Wait" in *Shout*; "Latover" in *The New Yorker*; "Look at
Her" in *Harper's Bazaar* under the title "You Captivate Me"; "Ravishing"
in *Gear*; "Los Feliz" in *Arena* and *Zoetrope: All Story*; "Whitecap" in
Harper's Bazaar.

Lines from "something for the touts" from *Burning in Water, Drowning in
Flames: Poems 1955-1973* by Charles Bukowski, Ecco/HarperCollins
Publishers, 1983, used by permission.

A CIP record for this book
is available from the British Library

ISBN 0–571–22123–8

10 9 8 7 6 5 4 3 2 1